MAKING SHADOWS

TONY McHUGH

For family & friends

To confront a person with his shadow is to show him his own light. Once one has experienced a few times what it is like to stand judgingly between the opposites, one begins to understand what is meant by the self. Anyone who perceives his shadow and his light simultaneously sees himself from two sides and thus gets in the middle.

Carl Jung, *Good And Evil In Analytical Psychology* (1959)

ACKNOWLEDGEMENT OF FIRST NATIONS PEOPLES

I proudly acknowledge First Nations Peoples – their stories, traditions, and living cultures on this land and its waterways. Furthermore, I respect and honour First Nations Elders, past and present, and look forward to an equitable and harmonious future for all. TM

CH 1 – LINH – FACE FIRST

Linh Nguyen had no idea she was about to die.

She was running late. And running late was something she didn't do. Usually, she was a well organised person, but on this particular Friday she had miscalculated. Maybe it was the extra food she needed for the family picnic. Maybe she should have written a list instead of trusting her memory. Her two girls would be waiting at the primary school pick-up. And as if to make matters worse, the operator at the checkout kept chatting to her friend in the next aisle while hovering over the register keys as if she was about to play a tune.

'Please hurry. My daughters get really anxious if I'm late. Don't bother putting it in separate bags, just throw it all in the one basket. It's already three-thirty. They'll be waiting.'

Linh snatched impatiently at the basket and rushed out to the carpark. There had been several upgrades at Birkenhead Shopping Centre over the past few weeks, and she hadn't noticed the 'Warning – No Entry' sign across the annexed area where she'd parked her vehicle. Just the same, she spotted her isolated SUV and thought she'd have no problem exiting into Roseby Street, as long as she was able to cross the makeshift barrier without disturbing the workers' equipment. She hadn't stopped running since she'd left the market. Up ahead, a man was leaning on the motor grader near her vehicle, and she guessed he must have been one of the workmen finishing up for the day. She hoped she wasn't going to get into trouble for parking in the wrong spot.

She kept shouting at the man that she was sorry. 'I didn't see the sign. Sorry. So sorry!' Still running. Out-of-breath. Her voice sounded hysterical.

The casually dressed figure had been waiting over an hour for a mystery-man by the name of Essie. So far, no show. He dropped his half-smoked cigarette on the ground and turned toward the fast-approaching woman. Just like he'd done in Nam, he panicked. A voice from years ago exploded inside his head. 'Grenade in basket!' Then another, 'Wait! Wait!'

He grabbed at the holster attached to his ankle and slid the knife from its pouch. As the screaming woman reached him, he wrenched the basket from her arms and threw it as far away as he could. His left hand gripped her nose and mouth. The other lunged and hacked forward in commando fashion. Mrs Linh Nguyen hit the ground face first. She was already dead. The man checked her for weapons, then brushed aside her hair to souvenir his kill. The contents of the basket remained scattered across the asphalt. Fruit, vegetables, packets of chips, nibbles – no explosives. Carpark B2 remained deserted. He dragged the slender body over to the Vinnies bin, pitched her over the rim and shut the lid. He couldn't wait any longer. Not now. His armoured personnel carrier would be waiting. Soon he would be safe. He would deal with Essie some other time.

CH 2 – BINDI – LAND OF THE DEAD

1952

Christmas Eve. Bindi screamed. Stopped. Held her breath and pressed down. Screamed again. And with each contraction the pain got worse.

She'd been taught by the Reverend York that the Virgin Mary had suffered a similar ordeal almost two millennia before. But that was scant consolation for this frightened Aboriginal teen. No Heavenly Father to believe in. No father of any kind to share the moment. No shepherds. No Magi. Just a makeshift bed. And hanging from its framework, a rolled towel onto which she gripped and pulled.

*

Mia, the go-to midwife, was well-practiced in the outback birthing routine. For years she'd been tending to the needs of the local community – a frequent occurrence now so many whitefellas from the south came and went. She looked down at the frightened Walpiri face, a face that resembled her own many years before. And she wondered what the young girl's story was. Wondered what her story would be.

With the next contraction, Mia saw a portion of the baby's head appear. It won't be long now, she thought. No need to call the doctor on Christmas Eve. She watched as Bindi let go of the towel for an instant, touching the infant's head for reassurance. But the hint of her smile was soon lost as the next contraction hit.

∗

For more than ten years, the Reverend Samuel York and his wife Elizabeth had run a mission on the edge of Katherine, a small town in the Northern Territory of Australia. And it was there they had employed Bindi as a gardener and sometime cleaner. When Bindi became pregnant, the pastor and his wife sought direction by praying to the Mother of God. They realised Bindi had sinned, for them that was undeniably true, but their faith led them to believe that forgiveness was the mainstay of Christianity. 'To err is human, to forgive divine' was an axiom they followed religiously, unless of course God's guidance led them to believe otherwise.

∗

Bindi's perineum began to tear. Then the whole head emerged. The shoulders were rotated, and the baby girl slid out. Mia was proud of herself. This had all gone to plan. She gave a nod to the silent figure looking on from the shadows, pausing long enough to see Mrs York make the sign of the cross not once, but several times, just to make sure the Eternal Father knew she really meant it.

The blood-streaked baby screamed an almighty scream, prompting a sigh of relief from the midwife. The cord was tied and cut. And after a brief look from Bindi, the baby girl was passed to Mrs York, who gently swaddled the infant and took her away.

Now for the afterbirth.

Ten minutes later there was another contraction. More of the placenta came away, but that was when Mia realised something was wrong. Bindi was exhausted, shivering, teeth chattering. Another contraction. Twins. And a breech! Mia began to panic.

For mother and midwife, the subsequent labour was long and arduous. A boy was born dead a day later. There had been severe haemorrhaging during the second birth. Mia was distressed, confused. Bindi stopped moaning an hour before she stopped breathing. The only doctor on duty arrived late Christmas Day – too late to save mother and child. Bindi lay there lifeless. Mia watched as the Yorks prayed over the empty body. She believed their prayers were meaningless. She knew, as her People knew, Bindi's spirit had already made its way to the Land of her Ancestors. The Land of the Dead.

*

'Your mother and brother are now with our Heavenly Father,' Mrs York told the baby girl. 'They rest in peace,' repeating the words her husband had often delivered from the pulpit.

Elizabeth and Samuel christened the baby girl Dorothy, named after Saint Dorothea of Caesarea. They thought it was an apt name for Bindi's child, given Dorothea was the patron saint of gardeners and midwives. But the couple knew important decisions had to be made. And weeks later, it was Elizabeth who pressed Samuel for a final answer. 'We need to plan what is best for God's little angel. Perhaps we should arrange foster care with a suitable Christian family in Darwin?' Samuel levelled an austere gaze at his wife and shook his head. 'Well then perhaps a religious institution in one of the southern cities?' Samuel shook his head again.

The pastor and his wife were well aware that, for decades, many of the local Indigenous children had followed this manner of removal and relocation. Regrettably, they also knew some were forcibly taken – many would say *stolen* – from their biological families for what faceless authorities considered to be the good of the child. Both Samuel and Elizabeth hesitated in allowing this to happen, because they were confident they knew who Dorothy's father was.

✶

In the weeks that followed, Dorothy was wet-nursed by Kirra, an Aboriginal fringe dweller who had just given birth to her fifth child. The arrangement was never meant to be permanent because the Yorks had already taken steps to track down a certain auburn-haired, blue-eyed water expert from Sydney who had periodically stayed at the York's house from January to April during the wet season. There could be no doubt that the timing of his stays coincided with Bindi's first trimester.

Elizabeth smoothed the corners of the document in her hand and turned to Samuel. 'We have all his contact details right here. He has to know about the consequences of his intimacy with Bindi. God knows, he has to embrace his Christian responsibilities.'

CH 3 – ALICE – ISOLATED

1941

Alice was fifteen when she waved goodbye to her father, Captain Donald Hewitt, or Dr Don, as his mates used to call him. It was February 1941. He was on his way to Singapore as part of the Australian Army Medical Corps. He wasn't alone. Australia had dispatched the Eighth Division of the AIF, four squadrons of the RAAF, and a contingent of eight warships.

Alice's mother Iris had feared this day would come, and despite Don's insistence he would be well away from front line fighting, she had a feeling he would never come back. Alice objected to her mother's pessimism. As far as she was concerned, her father was invincible and would always be there by her side to put things right. She reasoned it would only be a matter of time before he returned home to protect her, to love her.

1942

A year later, Singapore's 90,000-strong garrison of British, Australian, and Indian troops fell to the Japanese Imperial Army. More than 15,000 Australian soldiers were captured. Dr Don was one of the first to perish.

Alice could never accept her father's reported death. She became more and more irritable. Constantly quarrelling with her mother. Withdrawing from the few friends she had. Never seeming to be able to sleep for any length of time. Arguments broke out whenever her mother offered help. To relieve the tension Alice went for long walks alone. She began to smoke. Sometimes she would deliberately burn herself with a match or a lit cigarette butt. It was her way of gaining control, escaping her emotions by inflicting physical pain. Increasingly, the need for contrition and reparation began to take on an important part of her life. By some penitential shortcut, she thought she could bring her father back. If not his spent body, then at least a version of his life force.

Times for Alice and her mother were tough in the absence of their Dr Don. The rationing of basic commodities was introduced in May 1942. And those restrictions came only a month after the news of Don's death. Not only that, Alice was rudely awakened early on the morning of 8th of June. Sirens sounded all over the city. This time it wasn't a Japanese midget submarine attack. That was the week before. Right now, the radio was reporting that Sydney and Newcastle were being bombed. From her window, she could see searchlights waving around the skies, a bit like when *Gone with the Wind* came to town. Only at this moment she realised it was for a very different and potentially deadly reason.

'Put that bloody light out!' came the shout from the air raid warden, directed at Alice's window. Iris grabbed her daughter in an instant and hastened her into the hall. They'd been told the hallway was the safest place in the house because there were more walls between it and the outside. They'd already turned off the gas. And the bath was full of water in case there was a supply problem after the bombing.

Alice hugged her mother for the first time in a long while. They cried and laughed in unison under the mattresses, waiting for the bombs to fall.

Morning came with the news that Dover Heights and Newcastle

had been shelled by a Japanese submarine, the mother ship of the midget subs. No bombs had been dropped after all.

Daughter and mother should have been closer as a result of the shared mayhem, but paradoxically, and in some strange and twisted way, the shelling from the mother ship triggered in Alice a belief that her own mother posed an ongoing threat to her safety and wellbeing. And now, with her father no longer there to shelter her, she had to find a way to escape further danger. She would think about what she had to do. Plan it so no one would know.

1944

By 1944, the strain was beginning to tell on the Australian population at home. The Axis powers had effectively been overcome, but the war dragged on. Alice tried to avoid the newsstands on her way home from dressmaking class, but it was difficult to block out the fact that Australian troops were still being killed in New Guinea. Her spirits were down for lots of reasons. To start with, her clothes were drab. The shoes she had so treasured a short time ago were tattered from the combined effects of her long walks and the disintegration of the footpaths and city streets. On top of all that, she missed her father to the point of despair. She felt isolated despite her mother's presence. Isolated because of it. She plumped down on the couch in the living room, waiting for her mother's rebuke. About her mood. About her appearance. About her lack of respect. When it came, and she it knew it would, she would be ready for another confrontation.

1945

Finally, peace was proclaimed at nine o'clock on the morning of 15th of August 1945. Whistles blew. Strangers hugged and kissed each other on the street. The end of the war for Alice rekindled a yearning for another kind of attachment, one that didn't involve her mother. There had to be someone who would be the right one for her. She just knew it. One day, weeks after the armistice, she skipped her final week of dressmaking classes to welcome home the returning troops. She made her way out to Rose Bay flying boat base where a planeload of former POWs had just been flown in.

Alice was shocked by the appearance of some of the men. Several were emaciated. Their skin worse than the colour of death. She was so upset by what she saw it became impossible to hold back her tears. She was not the only one to cry. 'Shape up!' one of the nurses admonished her. 'Smile. Encourage our brave returning soldiers.' Alice courageously did so, and a few of the diggers tried to smile back. But to her they were no longer the young boys she had seen off on their way to Singapore. Bitterly, the war had turned them into infirm old men.

CH 4 – ALICE – THE PREMONITION

1945

It was Tuesday 6th November 1945. Alice waited at No. 2 wharf Walsh Bay for the RMS Circassia to berth. A hundred or more ex-POWs from Singapore would be on board.

She'd done this sort of thing before, walking the four miles from her home in Drummoyne to the city wharves. On previous occasions, she had welcomed the arrivals of the Arawa, the Duntroon, and the Highland Chieftain. And she'd gone back twice for the aircraft-carrier HMS Speaker, after its anticipated landing had been delayed due to one of the many strikes staged by the wharfies.

She scrutinised those coming ashore, looking for something or someone, she didn't know what. She recalled a recent newspaper article claiming that the returning POWs were cheery, normal Australians. It went on to fabricate that these men were not broken or even battered. And in body and spirit their scars had healed fast. But she knew these sorts of claims were just words. Propaganda for the masses. Years of malnutrition and all manner of tropical illnesses were unlikely to be erased in a matter of weeks. Nor would the spectre of years of constant physical and mental abuse by the Japanese be forgotten.

She'd come to grips with the fact that her father's body would remain *over there*, rotting in some unmarked grave. And yet she expected his spirit would return to her in some yet to be revealed way. When she saw the young lieutenant, she knew her instincts had been right.

He strode gallantly down the gangway and turned in her direction. He seemed to nod to her. Perhaps she was mistaken in this, but she was positive there was something about him she had seen before. In many ways, he reminded her of her father, at least how her father would have looked some fifteen or twenty years beforehand. She wanted to speak to him. To touch him. To make sure he wasn't an apparition. But just then, the young man and some of the other junior officers were ushered into a waiting bus. She realised they would spend the next few days at Ingleburn camp for a series of examinations and other formalities. Alice wished she could have gone with him, but she had a premonition there would be another time.

CH 5 – FRANK – A CUPPA

1922 - 1946

Francis Michael Keneally arrived in Sydney from Dublin at the age of three. His parents Connor and Winifred were desperate to escape the looming civil war in Ireland, and fashion a new life in Australia, a land they saw as a place of stability and opportunity. Connor was a trained journalist and gifted athlete, who would become a well-regarded sportswriter for the Sydney Morning Herald. Winnie, a milliner, made hats for a few of the local gift shops in and around Parramatta, where the couple initially rented a flat. Later, they moved closer to the city, leasing a small cottage in Drummoyne, not far from the parish church.

As Frank grew up, he became a keen sportsman himself, excelling in cricket and rugby league. But he also applied himself to his studies and did well enough in his Leaving Certificate to enable him to go to university on a scholarship. Eventually he completed a degree in civil engineering at the University of Sydney. Straight after graduation he went on to study at the School of Military Engineering at Liverpool, and then – much to his parent's anguish – was off to war as part of the Royal Australian Engineers force sent to Singapore and Malaya. Sadly, Connor, his father, died of a heart attack during his son's time as a POW in Changi.

Frank returned to his mother's Drummoyne cottage, a shadow of his former athletic self. Winnie nursed him back to a semblance of his pre-war bodily state, but could do little for his mental health, other than support and encourage him whenever she could. It would take a year before he was physically and mentally well enough to apply for a job with the Metropolitan Water, Sewerage and Drainage Board, where he was accepted as a junior engineer. Mother and son were in need of each other's love, but the scars of recent years remained for both of them.

*

Frank frequented St Mark's church during his year of convalescence, making a daily ritual of the stations of the cross. The feel of the wooden pews, the echo of his footsteps, and the smell of paraffin and incense gave him a certain solace from the misery of the last few years of starvation and torment. Through it all he continued to wrestle with his God, at the same time praising him.

Toward the end of his customary loop around the stations, he became aware of a young lady kneeling at the side altar. Twice she lit a full candle and dripped the molten wax along her forearm. She seemed not to have noticed him. He approached her. She wore a full length, light blue dress and a white scarf over her head. Beneath the scarf he could see wisps of blonde hair. Her face was a puzzle, delicate lips countered by desperate eyes. He remembered he had seen her a year or so ago on the Walsh Bay wharf when disembarking from the Circassia. She turned from her locus of homage, and, in that instant, she disarmed him. She placed the spent candle in one of the vacant holders, and let her loose sleeves fall to cover the wax encrusted blotches on her arms. She leaned forward and whispered, 'I'm dying for a cigarette. Can I bludge one?'

Frank was taken aback. 'Give me a few minutes. I've got three more to go. Then maybe we can chat out front.'

Outside the church she seemed a different person. Without the headscarf, she looked softer and less intimidating. 'I feel I've known you for a long time,' she said. 'Out of uniform you look like a normal, nice young man. Less grand perhaps, but also the sort of gent I would like to know better. My name's Alice, Alice Hewitt. I live in Day Street, just around the corner. Fancy us living so close together. You live in Tranmere Street, don't you? Walk me home.'

'Frank,' he mumbled. 'My name's Frank Keneally.' He almost forgot to tell her. He was acutely aware that it had been a long time since he'd spoken to a woman, apart from his mother and the nurses. He enjoyed walking beside her. Chatting to her. They ambled down Tranmere Street, took a left into Therry Street, and then came to a stop at a driveway that led to a carport and garage.

'This is where I live,' she said. 'We have two entrances at our place. One at the back for the cars, the plebs, and the unfit. And another at the front in Day Street. But that one's for royalty and mountain climbers. Come in and have a cuppa.'

Frank wondered why he took up Alice's invitation that day. What would have happened if he hadn't gone in? The backyard had a Hill's Hoist clothesline as its centrepiece. There was a path that led from the carport to the back door. A frangipani tree in one corner of the yard, a lemon tree in the other. The grassed area at the side of the clothesline would have made a great cricket pitch, or so Frank thought. Stepping inside, he came upon a sunroom, then a kitchen. 'Let me give you a tour to the front.' From the kitchen, there was a long central corridor with several rooms leading from it. The whole place smelt a little woody. Cedar perhaps. The corridor finally ran through to a curved veranda overlooking the Iron Cove Bridge, Rodd Island, and across the Parramatta River to Callan Park Hospital. Frank knew this as the lunatic asylum. A steep staircase led down from the veranda to a concrete path and wall. More steps continued down to Day Street, and then across to Brett Park. Frank could see why Alice thought the front was designed for mountain climbers. Retracing their steps back to the kitchen, a short, grey-haired, sinewy woman of indeterminate age had emerged from one of the bedrooms. Frank presumed her to be Alice's mother. She had the look of someone who was bearing the weight of the world on her shoulders.

'Mother, this is the gentleman from the Holy Name Society I was telling you about. His name is Francis Michael Keneally. Francis as in Francis of Assisi, and Michael after the warrior Archangel. Mr Keneally is a former army lieutenant and an engineer to boot.' Frank had not told Alice any of these things, apart from his first and last name. And he certainly didn't know Alice had previously spied on him outside his house, and again at seven o'clock mass at Holy Name. The whole thing unsettled him. Indeed, he began to realise that Alice knew more about him than he could have imagined. And he knew so very little about her.

'Pleased to meet you Mrs err … Hewitt.' He remembered Alice had introduced herself as Alice *Hewitt*.

'Alice is eighteen, Mr Keneally. And you are…?'

'Twenty-seven, Mrs Hewitt.'

Frank waited for another confronting question, but was relieved to hear, 'Do you have milk and sugar with your tea, Francis?'

'Yes I do, Mrs Hewitt. Thank you.'

'Call me Iris, Francis. And I will call you Frank.'

In the weeks to come it became evident to Frank that Iris and Alice did not have a loving mother-daughter relationship.

✳

'Mother! I'm going to the dance at the town hall tonight, whether you give your permission or not. The Americans will be there, and so will all my friends.'

Strange, thought Iris. To the best of her knowledge, Alice didn't have any friends. Iris didn't feel like fighting anymore. 'Please yourself. You always do.'

Alice was in the process of altering her best dress when the sewing machine jammed. She managed to fix the problem, but it took ages to pull the fabric free of the machine without shredding it. By the time she got to the venue in her mother's borrowed high heels, the military police were just leaving. 'What happened?' she asked one of the MPs as he was getting into his van.

'Nothing like adding a few drunk GIs to the mix,' he said.

'Yeah', a slurred voice came from shadows behind her. 'Fucking yanks spoiled a good night. The doorman shouldn't have let them in.'

A familiar face approached, pushing between Alice and the drunk. 'Frank!' she exclaimed. He led her home that evening and several evenings after that. They went to dances, fashion shows, movies. Alice couldn't believe how much Frank's mannerisms mirrored her father's. He spoke the same way. Even walked the same way – a good half stride more than her own. They made love for the first time when Winnie was away at a millinery workshop. Alice enjoyed having a certain power over him. Being able to get him to do what she wanted. She didn't see him as being weak, so much as being habitually accommodating. When she asked him to propose, she knew he wouldn't refuse.

Not long after Alice said 'yes', Frank asked Iris' permission for her daughter's hand in marriage. Iris could see her husband's kindness in Frank's blue eyes. He had the same jawline as Don, the same bushy eyebrows. He looked so much like her loving Dr D. Iris just couldn't work out why such a fine man like Frank would be interested in this troublesome offspring of hers.

✳

Looking past the embracing couple, Iris caught sight of her own image reflected in the glass window at the end of the hall. She had neglected herself for some time now. The lines in her face had got deeper. The rings around her eyes had grown darker. Her body was still slim, perhaps too slim. More importantly, she had stopped being happy. She hadn't thought about anything other than survival and death for so long, it had become a way of life. She had begun to forget things. Losing things. Forgetting names. Searching for words that didn't come.

Alice left the two of them while she went to pack some of her personal items. Alone with Frank, Iris had an instant desire to embrace him. She moved in closer. 'Alice is mad, you know. Honestly, I'm overjoyed for you to take her from me. You can have her. I had a talk with Don last night. He told me your marriage would ease my pain.' Frank did a double take on what she had just said. He didn't know if he should respond or let it go. Alice moved in with Frank that very day.

✳

The wedding a month later was a small affair. Frank's mother Winnie was there. Iris was absent. The police investigators determined that Alice's mother had accidently neglected to ignite the old gas heater in the loungeroom. Alone, she had nodded off on the sofa with the doors and windows closed. She had passed away in her sleep.

CH 6 – ALICE – THE SPIRAL

Alice and Frank waited until after they were married before moving to Day Street as a couple. It was a promise Frank had made to Father Kelly, the parish priest at St Mark's. When they finally did move in, Frank at first imagined he could smell gas throughout the house. It was, after all, only a short time since the tragic accident. In his mind Iris was still there, still nearby. And he was happy to feel it that way.

Alice, on the other hand, was quick to eliminate any trace of her mother's former presence. Iris' clothes were carted off to the Salvos. Other items not worth saving went to the tip. Sentimentality over her mother's keepsakes was lost on Alice, unless it was worth an immediate quid or two to put toward her home business as a seamstress. She set up her dressmaking supplies in a large room off the main corridor. Table, mannequin, sewing machine, textiles, fabric scissors, shears, and other such paraphernalia.

She also set aside a nursery room, one she hoped would be required soon enough. It was a smaller room between the main bedroom and the sewing room. Cot, change table, soft toys, ceiling mobiles. She realised Frank would be surprised by this newly designated room. Up until then, she'd given him no reason to suspect she was eager to have a child. When he asked her if there was something he should know, she shook her head. 'Not yet my love, but soon enough. I'm sure of it.' Frank knew she'd given up smoking too.

Joseph Francis Keneally was born almost a year later on the 21st of July 1948. He had curly whisps of chestnut hair with faint blond highlights. Winnie thought he looked like Frank when he was a baby, perhaps a touch fairer. Alice thought he looked more like her mother, a resemblance she didn't take kindly to at all.

Alice's problems escalated almost immediately after Joe's birth. She began to get shivers and aches, not only in her breasts but all over her body. Mastitis put a stop to breast feeding, and so baby Joe was bottle fed after the first week. Alice's mood swings worsened. She was anxious and irritable, and refused to eat for almost a week. Winnie moved from her own house to become a live-in carer, not only for baby Joe, but also for Alice, who had started having panic attacks resulting in episodes of self-harm. Thankfully, incidents like these dissipated by the time Joe was twelve months old. And, for a while, Frank thought the worst was over, and all would return to normal.

Alice's long walks seemed to help her. Sometimes she would be gone for hours on end, but then she would return joyful and eager to chat about the things she'd seen. Minor injuries on her legs and arms suggested she'd been trekking in the bushy area surrounding Iron Cove. Also, from the smell of her clothes, Winnie and Frank realised she'd taken up smoking again.

Not long after Joseph's birth, Alice and Frank took to sleeping in separate rooms. Frank didn't mind this arrangement at first, thinking it would only be temporary. Days led to weeks, then months. One Saturday morning Frank happened to walk into the main bedroom to empty the wastepaper bin. Alice quickly adjusted the blouse she was putting on, but not before Frank noticed several marks on her rib cage. At first, he didn't make any sense of them, but then he remembered he had seen similar wounds when he was a POW in Changi. Some of those wounds had been inflicted by the Japanese guards. Others, by the POWs themselves. The injuries were burns. He remembered Alice in church with the molten candle wax. And then he thought of the cigarettes.

Frank made the mistake of confronting her with what he had seen. An enraged Alice grabbed whatever was within reach and lunged at Frank with a pair of fabric shears that had been lying on the dresser. The attack was deflected successfully, but the likelihood of further danger to herself and to others prompted the family doctor to intervene and refer Alice for psychiatric assessment. She initially went to Gladesville Mental Hospital where she underwent electroconvulsive therapy over several weeks. During one of the electric shock sessions, her struggles to free herself from the restraints resulted in her sustaining a broken ankle, an injury not noticed at the time and therefore not immediately treated. A permanent limp resulted.

*

Alice returned to Day Street six months later, walking stick in hand and a smile on her face. 'They cured me,' she said. 'Where's my little angel?'

Frank had been working long hours for Metro Water, and in a relatively short span of time, had been promoted to a senior position. Winnie's presence and the care she provided had been a godsend.

Without her, baby Joe could have been taken to an institution. Winn was only too conscious of the fact that similar things had happened to others without family support.

With Alice back at Day Street, and Frank at work, it was just the two women and Joseph at home. Joe was now eighteen months old, walking the wobbly walk, talking the toddler talk. It was the summer of 1950.

Winnie provided support as best she could, but Alice remained remote and non-communicative most of the time. She would spend the daylight hours sitting on the veranda staring at the boats on the Parramatta River. She had also started reading about the mysteries of human consciousness. Winnie noticed she studied one particular book over and over again. It was called *Spiral of the Mind,* a self-help book about a meditative path that claimed to lead from outer perception to the inner soul. When Winn came to chat, Alice ignored her, displaying an unsettling outward calmness. Winnie didn't mind the silence as such, but she was sorry that Alice's ankle had put an end to the long walks she used to take. For Winn, a short time without Alice would have seemed like a holiday.

Often, during the day, Winnie would take a cup of tea out to Alice. It was one way of keeping an eye on her without being overly intrusive. On this occasion *Spiral of the Mind* had been abandoned on the empty chair. On the open page there was a diagram of a continuous spiral that looked like a coiled snake. The caption below the image claimed it represented the path from the demonic to the divine. Next to the spiral, Alice had scrawled '*My baby Joe is the devil incarnate. His gift to me is endless hell.*'

A baby's scream, and Winn knew where Alice was. There were spots of blood on the hallway carpet. Winn dashed into the baby's room. Alice had taken the fabric scissors to herself, cutting a deep spiral-shaped wound into her forehead. Blood covered most of her face. She was prodding Joe with a lit cigarette. Winnie grabbed the walking stick and repeatedly hit the arm that held the cigarette. At least that's what she did at first. Then she hit Alice anywhere she could. Without the stick for support, Alice stumbled to the front door. Winn ran after her. Another shuffle, and Alice's ankle gave way at the top of the steps. She fell awkwardly from the veranda to the concrete path, ricocheting off the sandstone buttresses and steel balustrades as she went. Winn stood on the veranda, looking at the misshapen figure at the foot of the steep descent. Alice's leg rested at an ungainly angle; shin bone protruded menacingly though the flesh. A pool of blood below her head grew by the second. Winn did an about-face and returned to Joe, calming him, tending to his wounds. She called the police. The police called Frank.

*

Frank got to the scene as quickly as he could, but by then Alice had been taken away. He was informed that his wife had sustained a severe skull fracture, as well as multiple injuries to her limbs, ribs, and internal organs. The medical team at Balmain Hospital did not expect her to live more than a few hours.

CH 7 – FRANK – THE PROMISE

Five years since the loss of Alice. Typical Saturday morning. Sydney summer. Smell of cut grass. Mr Whippy *Greensleeves* van. Drone of cicadas. Cricket in the park.

Joe was now almost seven years old. A blond, blue-eyed boy who loved his dad, his nanna, and his sport. The order was subject to change.

Frank sat in his study sorting through the week's mail. Most of it went into the bin, but there was one letter stamped from the Northern Territory that caught his interest. He anticipated it would be about the work he'd done there when seconded from Metro Water in the latter part of 1951 and early 1952 during the wet season. Back then, he'd been sent as a consultant to the town council of Katherine. Infrastructure for irrigation and water mitigation had been in urgent need of review, not only because of the occasional big dry, but also because of periodic flooding from the notoriously unpredictable Katherine River. Frank knew his recommendations for the levees had so far been ignored. He hoped this letter would provide a promising turnaround.

He was surprised to see that the letter was from the Reverend Samuel York, announcing he would be coming to Sydney in March for a meeting with the CEO of his mission. The Reverend wondered if they could catch up for a cup of tea at some stage during his visit. His wife's best wishes were also conveyed. Being a religious person

Frank had got on well with Elizabeth during his stays in Katherine. Indeed, he had been welcomed and accommodated by the Yorks on his frequent toing and froing over the course of a few months. Frank was delighted to be warmly remembered by the Yorks. He replied immediately, adding he would be honoured to lodge the Yorks at his house, if convenient. He also offered to show them some of the sights of Sydney if they had the time.

Samuel's reply came back a few weeks later, letting Frank know when he would be arriving at Kingsford-Smith airport. The Reverend explained that his time in Sydney would be a short one, but he would be happy to take Frank up on his offer for lodgings. His wife Elizabeth would not be joining him on the impending visit. Her presence at the mission could not be spared. The first two days would be spent on church business, but the third, on the Sunday would be free.

*

Frank immediately recognised the Reverend York as he walked across the tarmac. His black hat and clerical collar gave him a certain notoriety not evident for the other travellers.

'Francis, it's so good to see you again. It's been three years, hasn't it?' One more look at Frank – his jawline, his blue eyes – and the pastor knew he and Elizabeth had been right about Dorothy's father.

Much had happened in those preceding years. On the way back in the car, aside from the usual pleasantries, Frank outlined some – but not all – of the ups-and-downs that had occurred within his household during those uneasy times. He had decided he should do this in case the Reverend asked some awkward questions of Winnie and Joe during his visit. Samuel offered scant reply to what Frank was saying. Instead, he peered out the car window in awe, seemingly taken aback by the chaos of the big city.

Frank sighted the familiar two-person welcoming committee as soon as he turned into the back driveway.

'This is my mother, Mrs Winifred Keneally.'

'Please call me Winnie,' she said.

'And this is my son Joseph. He prefers Joe.'

Samuel politely shook hands with both of them before Frank led him to his room halfway down the hallway. 'Take your time, Samuel. It's already been a tiring day for you. Freshen up. Have a rest. Dinner is at seven, if that suits.'

The meal was kick-started with grace, courtesy of the Reverend. Conversations were made up of small talk. The humidity. The size of the city. The river. Nothing about the Territory or the Mission.

✶

The novelty of taking the bus to the city centre was not lost on Samuel. In some ways the magnitude of the city itself strengthened his resolve to request extra funding for his outback mission. As regards the other matter – the one about Dorothy – the kindness he'd been shown by the Keneallys softened his resolve to admonish Frank for his relationship with Bindi. Given the circumstances surrounding the mental illness and misadventure of his then wife a year or so before, Samuel understood why Frank may have sought female affection away from his normal locale and obligations. Samuel was also gratified by Frank's religious piety and his devotion to his son and mother. He believed this family would be the right one for Dorothy. He prayed for the strength to see it all through.

Friday and Saturday came and went quickly. Samuel was present in the Keneally household only briefly. Toast and jam, and a cup of tea for breakfast. Back for dinner, and then early to bed. The conversation was more congenial and relaxed on Saturday evening. Joe retired early following a long day playing with his friends. Samuel sat back, satisfied with his dealings with the mission's CEO, as well as certain other matters. He liked the Keneallys. All of them. And because of that he felt more confident about what was to come.

Samuel and Frank attended Sunday's early morning mass at St Mark's. Although not his denomination, Samuel reasoned that the Roman Catholics were close enough in the eyes of God. And the bonus of a traditional Latin mass was an interesting and intriguing embellishment to his own worship. He even contributed a small sum of money to the collection plate when Frank took it around.

*

After Mass, the two men strolled along the bay foreshore. At first there was silence, but Frank had an inkling that Samuel was about to raise a subject that had been playing upon his mind since his stint in Katherine. He got in first. 'How is Bindi? Has she asked about me?

Samuel hesitated. 'Perhaps we had better sit down.'

The pastor's words spread through Frank's body like an escalating electric current. *Twins. Bindi and the boy dead. Dorothy, Joe's half-sister.*

The news that Bindi could have been pregnant came out of the blue. Yes, Frank had spent a great deal of time with her, but they had only ever slept together the one time. And that had obviously been enough. A storm of thoughts rushed into his head. Of course, he would have supported her back then, if only he knew. Of course, he would love and provide for Dorothy as best he could now. He was financially secure, after all. And he felt sure Winnie would continue to be his rock. And Joe would have a young sister to protect. Frank voiced all these avowals to Samuel.

*

'I've been doing a lot more than dealing with the mission's head office, Francis. Dorothy's adoption papers were finalised yesterday, subject to your formal acceptance. As you probably know, the templates for this sort of arrangement for many of the Aboriginal children have been in place for quite some time.'

On the way back to Day Street, Samuel explained that Dorothy had spent the first six months of her life with Kirra, her wet nurse and carer. 'After her time with Kirra and her progeny, Elizabeth and I took Dorothy into our household, although she returned to the Aboriginal community on a regular basis to see her playmates. She speaks smatterings of the native Warlpiri language, you may be interested to know, although English as spoken by Elizabeth and myself is what she has been mainly exposed to. And believe me, her vocabulary is growing rapidly every day. Seriously, I believe she is acutely intelligent and has a beautiful nature.'

*

The next morning, Reverend York and Frank set off for the airport together. Winnie held Joe close to her as the two men prepared to depart. She had spent most of the previous night with her son. Listening to his story. Comforting him. Telling him how they could look forward to wonderful times together as a family. She conceded there were certain things that didn't need to be said – perhaps ever. It was a pact between them. It would be their secret until the time was right.

Frank paused before getting into the car. 'I'm going to bring back a surprise for you, Joe.' Joe's eyes lit up. He loved surprises.

CH 8 – JOE – NINE YEARS ON

1964

I recall the first time I saw Dot. I must have been six years of age. She would have been two. My dad had just come back from the Northern Territory with his promised surprise. Nan was in on it, but I had no idea what to expect. He lifted Dot from the car. Carried her to where nan Winn and I stood at the back door. And planted her on the ground in front of us.

Dad shouted out to me in a loud voice, 'Here she is Joe, your surprise!' Instead of running to nan and me, she skipped her way to the Hills Hoist and circled it several times before becoming giddy and falling over. She screamed and laughed, and we all laughed too. Nan was about to go and pick her up, but I beat her to it. I pulled my little sister up, and we stood looking at each other in a quizzical sort of way. Brown on white skin. Blue eyes on blue. Our bond was cemented then and there. And so it has remained.

We had early dinner that evening. Dot refused to sit in the highchair nan Win had used for my dad. Instead, she ate on the run, spilling bits of toast and cheese on the dining room floor. Something I would have been chastised for. Not long after that it became clear that dad's assurance she was toilet-trained had been premature. Nonetheless, that first day was one of the highlights of my life. Nan Winn and dad's too I suspect.

In the months that followed, Dot tagged along wherever I went. People used to say we were joined at the hip. I think in some ways we still are.

CH 9 – JOE – PSYCHOLOGY

I've just started a Bachelor of Arts degree at the University of Sydney. My aim is to major in clinical psychology, hopefully leading to a career as a psychotherapist. Well, at least that's the plan. But it wasn't always the way it was going to be until something happened that changed my way of thinking. Maybe that's why I'm doing what I'm doing now.

It was only a year ago. But it seems much longer. It was my final year of high school. I remember *House of the Rising Sun* was playing softly in the background while I continued my program of study leading up to the Leaving Certificate.

Nineteen sixty-five had been a mixed year for my cricketing aspirations. I hadn't batted well all the preceding summer, much to my own and my team-mates' disappointment. It was all something to do with my big back lift, and the coach hinted I'd have to do something about it in the off-season if I wanted to keep on as an opener. This had prompted a rationalised sporting retirement until the big exams were over.

Six hours of concentrated study had left me pretty much brain-dead by midnight. The girls had already gone to bed, and I was left in my self-imposed cocoon. My own bedroom-come-study and my father's bedroom shared a common wall, as did Dot's and Winn's. Boys at the front of the house. Girls at the back.

My dad had given me the larger bedroom when I was little. He told me that it was the only place all my toys would fit. Of course, I knew that the room had once belonged to my parents. From the window, I could look down to the road and across to the sloping parkland leading to the river. There were two pictures of my mother on the wall, one with dad, and the other by herself. Apart from these there were cricket photos and pennants, and a shelf of books and model planes. In contrast, the walls of my father's room were bare, apart from a crucifix above the bed.

I could hear him moving around in the next room. His routine hardly ever varied. Every night he would kneel by the open window and pray before getting into bed. He never shut the window, even in winter. He used to say the fresh air helped him think. Helped him sleep too. Through the open window there was a small passageway that divided the Keneallys from Miss Powderly's house next door. I liked the elderly spinster, and she liked me almost as much as her azaleas. I would often mow her lawn for a little pocket money or, even better, she would give me some freshly baked ANZAC biscuits. The other side of the house was where the Watsons had once lived. Their eerie old house had been knocked down and replaced by a block of flats.

I remember that night pretty well. I heard a knock on my bedroom door and realised dad had come to check on me. I'd already tidied my desk and had been sitting on the side of the bed, staring at the picture of my mother on the wall.

Dad asked me if I wanted a glass of milk before turning in.

I said I would, and thanked him.

When he returned with the milk, I thought I'd ask him why he became an engineer in the first place. Maybe he'd been planning to do that sort of thing for a long time before he went to university. Up until then I hadn't made any decisions about what I wanted to do after school. Obviously, my dad knew that. And perhaps he took that moment to put in another pitch for the sciences.

He said he didn't remember if he'd planned on being an engineer or not. He reckoned it just seemed easier for him to move in that direction. Then he asked me to seriously consider the sciences. I knew he would. I've never been that keen about physics and chemistry. And I told him so. He regarded me with an understanding tilt to his head – as he often does – and told me how happy he'd been at Metro Water. Then he said something about flood easements and drainage not being as bad as they sounded. I think he looked for a smile from me, but my mind was elsewhere. As my attention wandered, he said something about his job paying for the food on our table. Then he joked about it keeping him and me off the streets. I didn't react, which seemed to unsettle him a little. Then he asked me what I was inclined to do in the big wide world.

Up until then I'd told him I was thinking of being a schoolteacher. Maybe English and History. But then I dropped an absolute clanger. I said I was also thinking of going straight into the army.

I can't tell you how surprised I was to see my father's expression quickly change. His voice moved up a notch when he tried pointing out how teaching didn't mix well with the prospect of killing and being killed.

Then I was a complete smart arse, and reminded him that he'd never knowingly killed anyone himself.

His legs seemed to give way, and he sat down at my desk, searching for something to say. Unconsciously, he skimmed my notes on the tragedy of Macbeth. He became solemn. A tear trickled down the side of his face. I realised I'd touched on something I shouldn't have. Poor timing, I guess. I was about to apologise when he got up and left the room. I didn't know what I should do next. Then a few moments later, the former Lieutenant Francis Keneally returned with a dog-eared book. At first, I thought it was his New Testament, the one he keeps in the drawer of his bedside table. But then I realised it was something else. He flicked through the pages until he came to the spot he wanted. And then he read from his own handwritten record. I recall the exact passage. I know it pretty much word-for-word. It's cemented in my brain.

'At the start our experience with jungle warfare was limited. We learned to camouflage ourselves and move silently through the undergrowth. We were told that the Japanese soldiers were all short-sighted and they couldn't fight at night. That was all rubbish. They were formidable fighters, especially in the jungle. They had this knack of getting behind and around you. Often our troops were surrounded before they knew what was happening. We surrendered on 15th of February 1942. It had never occurred to me we would do that. They said it would save the remaining civilians in Singapore.'

My father shut the book and looked intently at me. He said something like, 'War isn't like it's portrayed in the movies.' Then he started reading again.

'We were part of "F" force when Singapore fell. The Japs herded us into railway trucks, then forced us to march at night through monsoonal rains. The Black Triangle guards beat us repeatedly with rifle butts and bamboo strips. We were down to six ounces of rice a day, and worked fourteen hours out of twenty-four, starting at 5 a.m.'

I hadn't moved a muscle since my father started reading. Somehow, I'd become paralysed by his words. And his face in those moments had become oddly less familiar. Then he opened his book again.

'We suffered from cholera, beriberi, typhus, dysentery, malaria, and tropical ulcers. Some of the leg ulcers used to get so bad the bone became exposed. The tendons would ripple when we moved. The flies would lay their eggs, and then the maggots would start wriggling around and feed on the marrow. Some of our soldiers would beg for their leg to be cut off. Sometimes this was done without anaesthetic. Sometimes it wasn't worth it. They died anyhow. Of the three and a half thousand Aussies originally in "F" force, a thousand died. The Brits fared worse, two thousand out of three thousand perished.'

My dad stood up, closed the book, and motioned towards the door. Then he stopped dead and swivelled to face me. 'I only spent the last year in Changi. Back home, that was the year my father died. The rest of my POW time I was all over the place.' Then he looked intently at me. And this is what he said.

'I try to convince myself that the experience didn't change the way I think about my fellow humans and my God. But I wrestle with both. I try not to brood, but I remember. Perhaps I'm more tolerant of other people's imperfections. Other people's hardships. Unless they're Japanese. That's a reaction I can't control. All I know is, when I got back and met your mother, I had a feeling that everything was going be all right.'

Then I blinked. He blinked. And the spell was broken. He apologised for rambling on. And then he went back into his room, probably to pray. I recall all this because I get why my father didn't want me joining the army. Maybe my degree in psychology will help me understand a whole lot of things about life, about living and dying, and about the things that make people do things. I hope so. At the moment, I don't have a clue.

CH 10 – DOT & TOM – WHAT'S YOUR NAME?

Thomas Patrick O'Leary was born on Boxing Day at King George Hospital for Mothers and Babies, Camperdown. It had been a relatively short, trouble-free labour. His mother and father were overjoyed. Edith and Albert had always wanted children, but parenthood had eluded them until the arrival of Tom. Edith was forty-two. Albert, fifty-two.

Tom was a ten-pounder with a Humphrey Bogart list to his mouth, and a beaky nose like his father. That didn't make him an immediate good looker to anyone but his parents. To them he was what they referred to as the bee's knees. He was eventually taken home to Drummoyne in a wicker basket made for the occasion twenty years previously by his now deceased grandfather Patrick. He was baptised at St Mark's Catholic Church, and eventually enrolled at the adjacent parish school.

Tom's first day at kindy proved to be an awkward occasion. He had started three weeks later than the other children due to a bout of bronchitis. He'd been dropped off at the gate wearing a blue and white sailor's outfit, lovingly pressed for the occasion by his mother. All the other children were in their grey and navy uniform. At the age of five, he was old enough to feel he was out of place. He sat in the corner of the playground feeling sorry for himself. Being alone was not unusual for Tom. As an only child he was used to it. Not that he liked it that much. Through bleary eyes, he watched the other children laughing, skipping, and running to the front of the building for assembly. He didn't know if he should join them or not.

'What's your name?' a self-assured voice came seemingly out of nowhere. He turned to face her. She had big blue eyes that made him dizzy if he looked at them for too long. 'My name's Dorothy Keneally, but my friends call me Dot.'

'My name's Thomas O'Leary. But you can call me Tommo.'

Dot took Tommo's hand and led him to line up with the others.

1958

Nan Winn wound the towel around her mischievous protégé and pulled. The spinning pirouette sent jets of water in every direction. Dot screamed with joy when she saw her nanna had been wet too. There was still another hour before dinner. Tonight, it would be steak and kidney pie.

Winnie called out to Frank, who was at that moment intent on listening to the radio in the loungeroom. 'Did you know Dot has a boyfriend at school? She says his name is Tommo, and I suspect there has been a bartering system going on with their food. I found the leftovers of a ham sandwich in Dot's lunchbox this afternoon. I know we didn't give her that today.'

Dot smiled and blushed but didn't contradict her nanna. 'I'm going to marry him one day,' was her only reply.

Winnie jumped when she heard the back door slam. 'What's for dinner?' Joe had just returned from playing park soccer with the girl next door. He'd triumphed again. Winn suspected Wendy always let him win, but she didn't dare say so. She knew Joe would rather have been playing with Wendy's older brother. But Steve 'Wotto' Watson, much to Joe's disappointment, spent most of his time after school playing footie and cricket with some of the older boys at the local public school.

Nan Winn didn't know much about the Watsons, other than what Joe told her. Apparently, there were eight Watson children. Seven of them girls. Wendy was Joe's age. She was the second youngest. The prettiest too, according to Joe. She also knew Joe used to sneak through a space in the backyard fence to shoot hoops with her, hoping Steve would join them. Joe didn't like Mrs Watson that much. He thought Mary, the eldest of the sisters, wasn't much chop either. One of them, sometimes both, would often call Wendy inside before the game had ended. Joe thought it was probably just to make him mad. Winn seldom saw the father. When she did, he always wore a white collar, black shirt, and black trousers. Wendy told Joe he was the minister at the local Protestant Church.

*

The steak and kidney pie had been a culinary delight for all. Dot told everyone it tasted just like wild possum and water python mixed together. Winn wasn't amused at her comment. Joe and Frank, on the other hand, were splitting their sides. Dot couldn't work out what they thought was so funny.

Frank cleaned up after dinner while Winnie searched her bookcase for another bedtime story. She had become intrigued with the magical tales of Aboriginal Dreamtime. Yesterday's story was about how kangaroos got their tails. Tonight's story would be about birds and their colours. Dot sat on the carpet near nan Winn's feet. Joe pretended to sand down his cricket bat, but he was listening too. He couldn't believe how many of the Dreamtime characters did really bad things. Some suffered because of what they did. But many of the others got away with what they did scot-free. And what puzzled him more than anything was the time sequence, or lack of it. There seemed to be no logical order between the past, the present, and the future. It all got shuffled, one into the other, until he couldn't work out if the story was in the here and now, or the there and then.

Joe put his bat down when nan Winn went to tuck Dot into bed. His curiosity kept him flicking through more of the stories. He stopped when he came to the picture of a giant Rainbow Snake. The story said it was the protector of water and the land, just like his dad.

CH 12 – TOM – THE GREEN CATECHISM

Tommo watched as Sister Jude drew pictures of angels and saints on the blackboard. Bit by bit, the dust from the multi-coloured pieces of chalk settled on her habit like twinkling stars in the Milky Way. Sister Jude was plump and surly, and her reddish cheeks grew even redder when she got mad, which was often. Some of the kids from the senior classes told Tom she was bald and had no tits. Of course, these stories were difficult to prove while her headpiece and habit were in place. Tits or no tits, it didn't really matter because Tommo, as well as all the other second graders, knew that the rules she laid down for being a good and holy Catholic would determine the path their souls would take in the afterlife. She told her class of seven-year-olds they had a choice. They could follow the rules laid down by the one true Church, and when they died, they would ascend straight into heaven. Or they could disobey, in which case they would plummet into hell and burn in everlasting fire.

Once a week, and twice during Lent, Sister Jude used to collect the children's pocket money for the black children in Africa. Tommo didn't think he was doing much harm then by taking up his own collection for Dot. She wasn't exactly African, but she *was* a little bit black. He would pocket half the proceeds as his commission and give the rest to Dot.

Dot worried that collecting all this money might be a sin, and so she bought holy cards with her proceeds and gave them out to her classmates. Tommo purchased lollies with his half of the loot and ate them himself.

None of the class seemed to be unhappy with the arrangement. It was one of those win-win things. The rest of the class got a share of God's-given grace for giving Tommo the money, and then they received an awesome holy card in the process. It had all gone without a hitch until Sister Jude found out about the scheme. She had suspected something sinister was going on because her own collections had recently become unduly meagre. One of the younger children had told her how easy it was to get a really good holy card for only a modest donation.

'Thomas. Come here!'

'Yes Sister.'

'Are you the one that's been organising collections for Dorothy?'

'Yes Sister. Do you want to contribute?'

Tom's little hands were beaten with the cane end of a feather duster. He was then bustled out of the classroom and locked in the hall broom closet for the rest of the day, which amounted to five long hours in searing heat. There among the brooms and the mops he contemplated what sort of sin he had committed. There was a possibility it might have been a mortal sin, because it had been serious enough for Sister Jude to beat him and lock him up. Then again, he had not done anything as bad as missing Mass on Sunday or eating meat on Fridays, therefore it might only be one of the venial variations.

Time passed slowly in the darkness and the heat. No fans. No air conditioning. To add to that, first thing that morning Tom had consumed a dozen jelly snakes, a sherbet, a bag of liquorice, and a bottle of Pepsi. After a few hours he had a full bladder and a sick tummy.

He was also beginning to worry about dying because he felt pretty bad. And what if he died now? He would not be in a state of grace. Perhaps he would never have a chance to get to heaven. Just in case, he thought it would be a good idea to say a perfect act of contrition. He did this before emptying the contents of his stomach into one of the buckets. Not all of the vomit was bang on target, so he had to wash some of it away into the corners with his wee.

Tommo had become the class hero by the time he was let out of the broom closet a few minutes before the final bell. The next day he was the school legend when it became obvious by the smell that the old cleaner had not rinsed out the bucket very well and had used the soiled mop to clean the main corridor.

As a result, Sister Jude devised the ultimate punishment. 'Thomas, I want you to gather the books from your desk and move across the classroom from the boys' half to the girls' half. If you like Dorothy so much, you can sit next to her for the rest of the year. She was an accomplice to your disobedience after all. And God has already seen fit to taint her in the bargain.'

Tom had noticed that Dorothy's twin desk always had a vacancy. He thought maybe she was too different for a lot of the girls to be friendly with. She was pretty smart. Perhaps too smart, and she showed it a bit too often. And of course, none of the class believed her when she told them she was not a new Australian.

'I want you to know that I'm not too thrilled to be here on the girls' side,' Tom confided. 'No offence to you of course. But I don't like the girls that much.'

'That's all right, Tommo. I don't like them much either!' Dot's broad smile made him smile too.

*

Preparations for the children's First Communion had commenced.

Who made the world? God made the world.

Who is God? God is the creator of Heaven and Earth and all things, seen and unseen. He is the supreme Lord of all.

How do we know there is a God? We know there is a God by the things he made.

How many Gods are there? There is but one God, who will reward the good and punish the wicked.

There was a knock on the classroom door. The children looked up from their green catechisms to see the short, round shape of Father Kelly shuffle into the room. Tom was amazed to see Sister Jude, the children's nemesis, blush in the presence of this plump, absent-minded priest.

'Well children, it's time for another practice. You must prepare to receive the Eucharist, the true body and blood of Our Lord Jesus Christ, who died on the cross for our sins. We want everything to go smoothly on the big day, you know. Now remember about your fast. You are not allowed to have food or drink for three hours before Communion, that is with the exception of water, which you may have at any time. Now, you children in the back, it's your turn this week to try the unconsecrated host.'

Where are true Christians found? True Christians are to be found only in the true Church.

What do you mean by the true Church? The true Church is the Holy Catholic Church.

*

Corpus et Sanguis Christi. Hoc est corpus meum. Albert O'Leary recited the holy words verbatim. He knew them all. Tom did too.

Albert parked the car around the corner from St Mark's and turned the engine off. 'Well Edith, our son's really growing up now. Do you feel nervous, Tom?'

'A bit hungry actually, but I'll be okay. I'm not going to be a sissy and faint. So don't worry about that. Just you make sure about mum. If she starts bawling, haul her out.'

'She'll be all right. A touch of holy water can do wonders. You run along now to the assembly, and we'll see you in church.'

'Do you have a clean handkerchief?' were Edith's parting words to her son. She turned to Albert seeking assurance. His strong, deeply lined face showed just a touch of rare emotion.

The couple got out of the car slowly, not forgetting Edith's carry bag with the camera inside. They walked arm-in-arm towards the front door of the church, nodding at the many familiar faces. Albert was proud to have Edith by his side. Edith was just shy of five feet, rotund, with a perpetually surprised look on her face as a result of her pencilled-in eyebrows. Albert, on the other hand, was tall and thin. He sported a thick head of mousy-brown hair, and his tiny upper lip was camouflaged by a moustache that looked similar to one of those furry caterpillars, the type that bleed green when they get squashed. Both were dressed in their finest. Albert wore his New South Wales cricket tie for the occasion. He loved his cricket almost as much as he loved his Catholicism.

Husband and wife dipped their fingers in the holy water font and blessed themselves, then solemnly walked down the central aisle to their designated pew, genuflected, side-shuffled in and knelt down to pray. Frank, Winnie, and Joe sat immediately behind them. A discreet widening of the eyes and a nod of the head by Edith to Winnie showed that the two ladies recognised each other from the after-school pickup.

Although normally frowned upon, Father Kelly had given his permission to allow cameras into the church to be used for the children's entrance only. After that, no pictures were permitted. Albert could see Edith was at the ready. The organ music began, and a few minutes later, the angels arrived, girl and boy, two-by-two. The girls looked like Christ's little brides, complete with miniature wedding dresses and veils. The boys were outfitted in navy suits, some with their hair in place for the very first time, neatly slicked down with their father's Brylcreem. With prayer books and rosary beads clutched in their sweaty, little hands, they sought out their respective families.

Albert gave Edith the signal. Her finger tensed, ready to press the camera button. Then it froze. There, second from the front, was their cherished Tom. Next to him was Dot, her dark skin contrasted against the snow-white dress. Albert nudged Edith, but she continued to hesitate. The moment passed. Edith kept standing long after she was supposed to sit.

Albert seemed concerned. 'You better sit down, Edith. Are you feeling all right? You've gone completely white.'

'Of all the times the camera had to jam. Sorry my love,' she whispered.

Just then Frank leant forward from the row behind. 'Couldn't help but overhear. You can have one of our shots. We've got plenty.'

CH 13 – WINNIE – THE SNAKE PIT

1964

Winnie wandered through the grounds of Callan Park. Pausing, she looked across to Rodd Island and then beyond to the houses sprinkled like confetti on the opposite shore. She found it difficult to reconcile what many failed to realise, that the beauty before her betrayed the presence of a dendritic network of lunacy. Sense and absurdity were shrouded there, inside and outside the borders of the asylum.

She turned her head in the direction of the screaming. High on the hill above the cricket fields, she watched as the inmates played their own kind of game. The man in the middle remained still. The others shed their clothes and threw them over the enclosure's wire fencing. They ran around the motionless man, shrieking at the top of their voices until an attendant turned a high-pressure hose on them. The centre-man then sprang to life and took his opportunity to scale the fence, only to be targeted by the same guard with the hose. Winnie wondered if the aspiring escapee would ever be able to cope with the freedom he sought.

Winnie had just been to visit her daughter-in-law. She performed this ritual at least once a month, sometimes more often. For almost fifteen years, she had guarded the secret. At times, she viewed it as a penance. At other times, she did it as an expression of love for her beautiful grandson. Her own son, Frank, on the other hand, could never bring himself to see his wife ever again. Winn understood.

All those years ago, there had been little hope Alice would survive past the first day. Miraculously, her body had been splinted, stitched, and stapled into a semblance of physical normality, apart from the limp and facial mutilation. Her mind, however, had been deemed beyond repair.

Winn reflected on the story as it had been told to her – how the doctors at first tried insulin-coma therapy, then more shock therapy. At one stage, they even contemplated performing a prefrontal lobotomy, but this approach had been shelved when the new generation of antipsychotic medications started to take effect. Thankfully, Alice's agitation and aggression slowed, then stopped – replaced by limb rigidity and a Parkinsonian tremor. And Peace.

Winnie came to learn that Alice had not shown any inclination to harm herself, or anyone else for that matter, for quite some time. In fact, the medical staff allowed her to roam the asylum grounds unsupervised, provided her medications continued to be effective. That's when Winnie started visiting her. Alice and Winn would often stroll along the boundary of the cricket fields. From time to time, they even ventured closer to the river. Sometimes they spoke. Sometimes it was a silent pilgrimage.

Today's visit was much like the others. Winnie had watched the ageing Alice stumble along with her walking stick, occasionally stopping to poke into shrubbery and hedges, under seats and benches. Always whispering to Winn that she was looking for her baby boy.

Winnie stayed a little longer on this particular day. She sat by herself on one of the park benches lazily watching the cricket. One of her friends had told her that watching cricket was like watching the grass grow. But she enjoyed the rhythm and the movement of the players. And her grandson Joe was a cricket tragic. She loved his enthusiasm for the game. Occasionally, she lifted her head to the sky and stretched. She could see the faint crescent of the moon as it appeared through whisps of clouds. And she wondered what this snake pit of an asylum would look like when viewed from another celestial body. Would the terrain look any different than anywhere else on Earth?

Winnie accepted that better times and worse times would come and go in the approaching years. One day she expected she would receive word of Alice's death. In some ways it would be a blessing. She thought it would come soon enough.

CH 14 – JOE – THE HEADSTONE

1966

I used to visit my mother's grave every year around the time of her birthday – with my dad, nan Winn, and Dot. The headstone reads: *Alice Enez Keneally 1926-1950. Loving wife of Francis. Devoted Mother of Joseph. Gone too soon. Until we meet again.*

Being there with Dot, and seeing the headstone, I realise I miss my mother in a different way than Dot. I at least know what my mum looked like. Where she's buried. But Dot has no idea what her parents were like. No-one seems to know who her real father is or was.

The way I figure it, Dot has an emptiness that isn't totally due to the loss of her mother. In some ways her Indigenous culture has been lost too. She doesn't know much about either one. There has to be a lot more to it than hearing about rainbows and serpents, or learning about nature, spirit, and the land by reading or listening to simple stories.

CH 15 – JOE – PASTOR JOHN

I'm now in my second year of psych, but I still can't get my head around one of the things I experienced as a kid. So I'm writing it down now, and maybe by the end of my course I'll be able to unravel it. It involves the Watsons, our next-door neighbours in Day Street.

There were ten of them. Reverend John, his wife Elva, and eight children. Seven of the children were girls ranging from around five to eighteen years of age. One of the girls was Wendy. Same age as I was. I used to play soccer and netball with her off and on. The only boy was Steve, a couple of years older than me. He was good at all kinds of sport, especially cricket. He was a top batsman. A bit of a tonka at times. At other times he could stick around all day. I called him Wotto. I wanted to play with him more often, but he kept hanging out with guys his own age.

Anyway, we both ended up playing for Balmain District Cricket Club. I was in the under 14s. Wotto was in the under 16s. It was a Saturday. All the district cricket teams usually met early at Drummoyne Oval before being transported to their respective venues. On this particular Saturday the 14s and 16s were due to play Balmain Police Boys Club. The PBs had pretty strong teams, and games with them were always close contests. But this day's games were cancelled at the last minute as a mark of respect for a young policeman. He was killed the night before, outside Balmain Leagues Club trying to break up a fight. Both teams were given equal points as if our matches were drawn.

Before trudging with the kits back to Day Street, Wotto and I did some net practice at the oval. I was a pretty good leg spinner then, and I troubled him on several occasions. Up to this stage he hadn't spoken to me much, but that day we had lots to say to each other. It was still early in the day, and Wotto and I weren't expected back home until late afternoon. Our net practice went so well I thought we might continue with a game in my own backyard. I'd mowed a fresh playing strip the day before to act as a pitch to practice my leggies. And I wanted to try it out on Wotto. But by the time we got back, he wasn't that interested in more cricket. Instead, he said he could show me the dungeon under his house. I had a thing for horror stories at that time, so the sight of a real dungeon sounded pretty awesome. In fact, Dot and I used to joke that the Watson's old two-storey house was haunted. The upper level even had a structure that projected out of it like a medieval castle turret.

Anyway, Wotto and I chucked our bats and kitbags on the back porch of my house, went down to the end of the backyard, removed the usual fence palings, and snuck up to the side of the Watson's house. Even though Wotto knew where a key was hidden to open the front door, he wanted to show me the secret entrance to the dungeon. He pointed to a small wooden gateway cut into the sandstone, about two feet by three feet, secured by two latches. He assured me this was the best way in. The wooden hatch was covered with cobwebs and mould, which made it truly believable as the door leading to a dungeon. We managed to squeeze through the small opening, but once inside the space was big enough to stand upright, maybe with a foot or two to spare. Although it was dark, we could still see because of the streams of light that came in through vent holes in the sandstone exterior.

Along the internal walls, there were frames for shelves and bedding, which Wotto told me had been put there in case the lower level needed to be used as a bomb shelter during the war. He pointed to a ladder leading up to a trapdoor. This was where we could get into the rest of the house. Up until this point, I was having lots of fun. We exited the cellar-come-dungeon-come-bomb shelter through a trapdoor which led to a storage room under the stairs. I pretended it was part of a commando raid spying on government secrets.

Almost immediately, we heard a voice coming from a room further down the hall. It turned out to be the kitchen. We crept along the carpeted floor and stopped in a nook opposite a partially open door. The pastor's booming voice could be clearly heard. He said something about his wife disobeying him. And he had sanctified her by punishing her daughters in front of her.

I have since looked up the piece in the bible. He'd been quoting from *Ephesians 5*.

It reads: '*Wives, submit to your husbands, as to the Lord. For the husband is the head of the wife even as Christ is the head of the Church … Now as the Church submits to Christ, so also wives should submit in everything to their husbands.*'

Wotto and I kept peering in, not knowing what was going on. This is what we saw.

We saw the Reverend John, outfitted in his white clerical collar, black shirt, black pants, black shoes. A black leather strap in his hand.

We saw Mrs Watson, black scarf around her head, tears running down her face, dressed in a neck to floor heavy black smock.

We saw all seven daughters lined up along the kitchen benches. All were naked. Some had ugly red weals on their lily-white skin. Wendy, in particular, looked like she'd taken a full-on hiding on her back and buttocks.

The Reverend was about to unleash on one of the older sisters when he sensed he was being watched. In that instant, he caught a fleeting glimpse of his son. Wotto banged the door shut, and we both ran down the hall. I went down the hatch first. It was too late for Wotto, who courageously fastened the trapdoor above me, and ran into an adjacent room as a diversion. I stayed there on the ladder for what seemed like an eternity, listening to the minister strapping the hell out of his son. I have also looked up the passage Rev. John was quoting from. It was from *Proverbs 3*.

'My son, do not reject the discipline of the Lord
Or loathe His reproof,
For whom the Lord loves He reproves,
Even as a father corrects the son in whom he delights.'

I eventually escaped the way I came in, secured the latches, and careered through the gap in the fence, replacing all the loose palings. It seems Wotto never let on I was there with him. And his father never suspected there were two of us.

That night I returned Wotto's bat and kitbag to somewhere he would find it. I never had a chance to speak to him again, although I occasionally saw him on his way to and from school and church. His sister Wendy never came around again either. A month later the family left the district – lock, stock, and barrel. I found out they didn't own the house after all. They rented it from the church. The premises lay vacant for a year or so, and then the whole house was knocked down and replaced by a block of flats. I've never mentioned what happened that day to anyone. Not anyone. This is the first time I've written it down, but not the first time I've grappled with it in my head.

CH 16 – JOE – STREETWISE MARGOT

I'm enjoying second year at university, although the deadlines and exams don't turn me on that much. But I guess they are part of the package, after all. The lectures are pretty interesting, especially *Abnormal Psychology*. That subject makes my head spin, which I like. Just the same, I'm taking a break from my unfinished assignment to set free some of the things that are clogging my brain. Getting them onto a page, so I can move on. At least that's what my psych theory tells me to do.

Margot Jarvis is the culprit. I met her in first year. She's a genius at statistics. She started a year before me, in '65, but then took the rest of the year off because her parents got killed in a light plane crash. Some mechanical fault, and it nose-dived into the bush while they were on their way from Goulburn to Sydney. They were livestock managers at a cattle farm outside the main town. Her parents also had a city pad in Surry Hills. A sizeable apartment too. That's where she lives now. It's hers. She was an only child.

She didn't withdraw into a shell after the accident. She reckoned she got through her grief by spending her time doing charity work and helping out at Redfern Community Centre – doing activities with the Aboriginal children after school. One time she made up a program called *'I Spy'* where she took the kids on photographic excursions. Got the photos developed in hard copy, then spent hours and hours writing down what they told her about the photos. She was gobsmacked by their stories. Then she turned the photos and stories into an exhibition at the Centre. Lots of people came. Changed the way people thought about the place – the community too. The Sydney Morning Herald picked up on what she'd done and published it as a feature article. I remember reading it and wondering at the time if she was going to do another project like it. Maybe I could help. But the local council canned it. Said it was way too expense, even though it cost them almost nothing. Then I found out the same Margot was in my psych class. She is truly amazing.

We used to hang out on campus a lot of the time. At first it wasn't like she was a regular girlfriend or anything. I went out with other girls back in first year. Some of them continued on from when I went out with them at school. But there's something different about Margot. She's streetwise and has a worldliness that blows me away. Some of my mates reckon she looks like Cher. I guess she does when she dresses in her hippie gear. Tall. Long black hair. And she sings too, but not in the same way as Cher. More like a white Diana Ross.

Anyway, we seem to have progressed past the platonic friendship stage. I spend Fridays and Saturdays at her place. It's not only sex. It's a lot more. Sometimes I help her pack food parcels at the nearby Wayside Chapel for the homeless. Sometimes we just sit in the park and read. I can't believe she's been living in the apartment by herself. Now she's hinting that maybe I should move in with her. Maybe I should. But I don't want to rock the boat at home either. My sister Dot wouldn't take it so well. Dad and Winn too. But then there is this strange sort of uneasiness when I'm not with her.

CH 17 – DOT – DANCE & DREAM

1968

Dot loved to dance. She took delight in performing her own versions of the *Silent Snake* and the *Kangaroo Dance* not long after she could walk. But she had never taken formal *contemporary* classes until recently.

She knew she didn't have balletic proportions. But she'd been told by her teacher and others in the class that she had a certain freedom of expression and underlying strength that made her movements exciting to watch. *Creative* was her favourite style.

'Body, action, space, time, energy,' she could hear her teacher's voice. She kept pushing through the pain in her legs and feet. She stretched with her back on the floor, one leg extending high into the air. She assumed the form of an emu, only to be immersed in an imaginary cloud of dust. Her teacher's voice faded away, replaced by another sound. She could hear the rhythmic beating of the electric fan, over and over. Over and over. The beating of the songman's sticks. Click, click, click. Drrr-rrr. The didgeridoo playing to the beating of the sticks, then changing to the rhythm of the song. Then back to the beat of the sticks, and on to the stomping of feet on dry earth.

Dot kept on with continuous movements – running, springing, hopping, jumping, gliding, rotating, flying. Her actions were separate, and yet one fluid syncopation. She stopped. The spontaneous applause from the other members of the class embarrassed her. She looked to her dance teacher for reprieve. She too was clapping.

✳

'Those outback chicks really know what it's for and how to use it. They love it Tommo. They really love it.'

Pete Cuthbert was boasting about his latest carnal exploits over the Christmas holidays. Tom listened, not believing it all. And yet his fifteen-year-old brain had become increasingly interested in the ins and outs of sex. He was well read on the techniques of *making it*, but he hadn't exactly *done it* yet.

Tom really didn't like Pete that much, but he secretly admired his baser accomplishments. Pete was two years older than Tom. He'd had it off with Kay for sure. Apparently, he'd scored with a few others as well. If what he said was anywhere near the truth, his exploits during the Christmas holidays had been another raging success.

'They bang like a dunny door on a windy night mate! Mind you, I wouldn't be seen dead in the light of day with any of them. But that doesn't seem to worry them much. Some of them even reckon a white fella like me is better at pointing the bone than their own kind.'

Tom kept thinking about Dot. He wondered if she'd done *it* yet. He wondered if she would do *it* with him. They hadn't talked much with each other since he'd left St Mark's to go to the Brothers school. They saw each other occasionally at Mass, but Dot stayed with her family, and Tom stayed with his.

✳

That night, Tom dreamed of Dot.

He peered over the top of her bed. Was she asleep still? He couldn't tell. The only light came from the reflection of the half-moon on the mirror. He bent down to feel her breath on his face. He shivered. It was sweet, like she had a dollop of honey on her tongue. She rolled on her side for a few seconds, then onto her back. His erection pulsated in his hand like a throbbing python. Quickly, he pulled down his boxer shorts.

He bent down again. Her smell excited him. His pulse was racing. He gently nibbled her ear, just at the place where he'd read it would have maximum effect. She gave out a little moan and partially opened her eyes, then closed them again as if she didn't want to escape from the dream.

Tom became bolder next time, and cushioned his mouth on her slightly parted lips. He let his tongue touch the area inside her upper teeth and quickly withdrew.

Did he imagine her tongue followed his?

He kissed her again. This time he penetrated beyond her teeth. She returned his advances and let out a soft whispering sound. He lifted his body cautiously under the bedclothes and nestled his pelvis in beside her buttocks. She immediately swivelled to face him, not with alarm, but with acceptance. Her nightdress had lifted to just under her armpits. He knelt with the bedclothes covering his shoulders, forming a little tent. She was now on her back with her legs wide apart. Her hands cupped his buttocks and pulled him down. They kissed passionately.

She was wet when he entered her. She possessed him totally. This was not the way Pete had described it. When they came, they came as one. She let out a muffled cry. His was loud and lasted a lot longer.

'Are you all right in there, Tom?' His mother's voice emanated from the next bedroom.

'Yeah mum. Thanks, I'm fine. Just another cramp. I'll stretch and give it a rub. It'll go away. I'm sorry if I woke you both.'

'Don't worry about your father Tom. He's still asleep. Listen to him snore!'

Tom listened carefully. He could still hear Dot's exhalations. The T-shirt he had carefully moulded around the end of his penis was sopping. So were his sheets. By morning they would dry as they always did, in a starchy sort of way.

He was thinking he should go and wash his hands. He had read somewhere that cum could give you warts. He already had a couple on his right hand that were obvious enough for all and sundry to see. He hoped no-one would know how he got them.

*

Tom hesitated outside the confessional. He could see that 'Farter' McGee was on duty. There was hardly anyone around so he thought he would go straight in and get it over with. Inside, he could hear the prayer book promptly close. The priest was obviously having a lean time that afternoon. He slid the latticed partition open. The smell hit Tom like a bin full of rotting vegetables. It must have been unbearable inside the priest's enclosure!

'Bless me Father ...' Father McGee prompted.

'Oh. Sorry, Father. Bless me Father for I have sinned. It has been a month since my last confession. I have been disrespectful to my parents twice. I have had impure thoughts several times. I have committed self-abuse four times. And I have told lies twice. Make that three times. For these and all my other sins I am deeply sorry.'

Tom was surprised and relieved when the priest handed out a lenient sentence. Four Our Fathers and two Hail Marys, and without cross-examination like he sometimes did. He felt sure Father McGee liked hearing the dirty bits when he was in the mood. An act of contrition was duly said, and Tom was out before the priest let the next one go.

CH 18 – BATMAN – PEACE?

1968

The pink Volkswagen beetle screamed to a halt at the traffic lights. Its long-haired driver had worked his butt off for the last few uni holidays to buy her. The sticker across the rear window spelled out PEACE. A flower-power sticker was affixed to the bumper bar. The VW was deemed female. Her hackneyed given name was *Venus the Love Bug.* If the observer was high enough in elevation or on weed, he or she would see VENUS painted on her roof.

Joe sang *We're Sgt Pepper's Lonely Hearts Club Band.* It was the final year of his degree. The traffic lights turned green, but before he could take off, a ragged-looking dude with a beard, fringed hippie vest, and a Che Guevara black beret stepped out in front of him, blocking his way. Joe wound down the window and was about to abuse him when the flower child raised his hand and shouted, 'Peace?' A question, rather than a statement. A cricket bat was in his other hand.

Joe inched past him with care and frustration. No sooner was he clear when there was a crash on the back of the car. '*War* is Peace, man!' Another crash, and the rear window caved in.

'Fuck!' was Joe's only audible reply. The black-bereted aggressor sprinted across the road and down an alleyway. Joe's rage took over. He floored the accelerator and whizzed around the block in no time flat. It only took a single circuit before his target was sighted sitting with his back propped up against a shop front, lighting a cigarette.

Joe was determined to exact revenge. Venus mounted the curb and continued along the footpath. He was only a matter of metres from his intended target when he snapped back to reality and realised what he was about to do. The black bereted man had recovered enough to use his cricket bat as a veneer of protection. But a raised piece of English willow was poor defence against the love bug's kiss of death.

The VW burned to a stop. Joe looked down at the face of resignation. The Batman raised his right hand and nestled the tip of his index finger to his temple, then bent his thumb feigning a hole-in-the-head manoeuvre.

Venus backed up, burped a backfire and scraped onto the road again. This time, heading in a new direction, away from the university, away from the day's classes. An hour later, Joe parked between two familiar camphor laurels. He was still shaken. What just happened didn't make sense! He got out of the car and inspected Venus' rear end. No window. No PEACE. Joe shook his head and tried to laugh. No sound emerged. Just a lot of nothingness.

*

The cemetery was crispy cool even though it was mid-morning. Mist rose as sunlight shone through shifting branches of moulting trees. Joe straddled the fence effortlessly and sauntered, hands in pockets, to the place where he would make his next decision. He sat on the low boundary wall and shielded the glare from his eyes while he made a cursory inspection of the place he had once visited regularly with his father, his nanna, and his sister.

The two headstones in the family plot at St Patrick's were stalwart and looked as though they would last a century or more. A few of the surrounding memorials had already done so, dating back to the mid-1800s. Unlike the adjacent weathered slabs, this pair stood proud and largely unmarked. One of the headstones read, *'In the midst of life we are in death.'* Below this, in the same style of writing, *'Iris Victoria Hewitt 1903-1947. Wife of Donald (dec.). Mother of Alice (dec.). Rest in Peace.'*

The other headstone read, *'Alice Enez Keneally 1926-1950. Loving wife of Francis. Devoted Mother of Joseph. Gone too soon. Until we meet again.'*

Joe reflected on the dates. His mother hadn't been much older than what he was now. He looked back in the direction of the memorial, but a shifting beam of sunlight led him to a nearby older gravestone. The inscription was in the classical style of the nineteenth century. *Man is made by his beliefs. As he believes, so he is.* Instinctively, the episode with the hippie had drawn him back to this place of reverie. He kept asking himself. *What* did he truly believe in? *Who* did he truly believe in?

A quickening of the breeze took his attention away from the graves. Once again, the glare through the shifting trees was blinding. He tried to shut the light out with an improvised salute, but when he returned to the headstones his eyes retained vignetted after-images of his mother's face. He imagined he could see her lying there, her face just the same as in the picture on his bedroom wall. He spoke to her. 'I nearly killed someone today, not by accident either. The man with the bat would have been a victim of my inner rage. My lecturers would say I'm having an existential crisis. What do you think? What does it all mean?' He pondered the words on the old headstone as the image of his mother faded and transformed into another face.

It was Margot.

CH 19 – JOE – THE BALLOT

I've left Day Street and moved in with Margot at her Surry Hills apartment. It's big compared to most in the area. It's a three-bedder on the second floor overlooking Prince Alfred Park and Central Railway Station. *Venus* is resting at Day Street while her back window gets replaced. A weird hippie shouting 'War is Peace' smashed it in the other day with a cricket bat. Apparently, he's only doing that to cars in the area with PEACE stickers. Which is a lot of cars. Maybe he's a Vietnam Vet, because the word is he wears the black beret of the Royal Australian Armoured Corps. He wasn't championing Che Guevara after all. I reckon this guy and Che are living on borrowed time.

Anyway, it looks like I won't be needing my car for a while. Parking in Surry Hills is a nightmare, and transport is pretty good. If dad can work out the angle of the pedals on the VW, he can try her out, although I know he's going to baulk at driving around in a pink car.

And Margot. I've fallen in love with her. She seems headed towards being an epidemiologist, whereas I'm more into therapy. She has this habit of sauntering over to my desk at Fisher Library. Disturbing me. Happy to be disturbed, I guess. Today she was wearing a micro-mini, black stockings with suspenders, and a tight anti-war T-shirt. How am I supposed to get any work done when she comes over like that and then sits on my notes?

Anyway, I'm finding it hard at the moment to concentrate on anything related to my studies because I have to register for the conscription lottery. They call it the National Service Ballot. I turn twenty on 21st July. If my marble gets chosen, it may solve a lot of the problems about what I'm going to do next. My lottery prize would be two years full time in the Australian army, followed by three or so years part-time in the Reserve. Dad's not too keen on any of this. Neither is Margot.

*

I've now completed my registration at the Department of Labour and National Service (DLNS). I get a Certificate (note the capital 'C') for doing this! My birthday goes on file for the ballot.

Then it says:

You must immediately sign this Certificate in the place indicated and keep it as evidence of your registration. You may be required to produce it to persons authorised under the Act. It must not be altered or defaced.

If the details shown on this Certificate are incorrect, or if you lose this Certificate, or if it is destroyed or defaced, you must report the fact forthwith to the Registrar below.

If your place of living changes from that shown in your registered address, you must advise the Registrar below within 30 days and return this Certificate to him as indicated on the other side of this Certificate.

I read the rest of the fine print, but it doesn't worry me that much. Some of the people I used to know at uni burnt their cards and went bush. Not me. Let the ballot decide. If the July 21st marble comes out, so be it. I'll tell dad and Margot that all I'll be doing is complying with the law. If my chance to go to Vietnam comes up, I'll take that too. But for reasons other than what the Government would have me and the other nashos believe.

*

The results of the National Service Ballot have been posted. And the lucky numbers are:

July 3, **21**, 22, 24, 30
August 1, 3, 16, 18, 24, 26
September 5, 9, 12, 14, 22, 23, 24, 26
October 3, 13, 18
November 5, 18, 24, 28, 29
December 7, 12, 14, 15, 19, 21, 22, 26.

I win!

CH 20 – HOPS – THE MOTH

1968

Joe's temporary deferment from National Service would only last until the end of the academic year. First degree completed, he would then need to present himself for the usual preliminaries including physical examinations, chest x-rays, urine analysis, interviews, and security checks. But all that was still a few months away.

Today, he attended a rally on the front lawn between Fisher and the quad. It was freezing cold weather for the start of spring. A light drizzle fell. There was a small but devoted crowd listening to the ear-piercing words of the speaker.

The Government is conscripting our men to kill and die in a war that has nothing to do with us. We must let the Australian Parliament and the gods in the White House know that the Australian people are not all the way with LBJ. We do not condone napalming of women and children. We do not condone the bombing of cities and villages. We do not condone the destruction of forests by tactical use of Rainbow Herbicides. And apart from damage to the environment, who knows what harm these dioxins like Agent Orange are doing to innocent villagers. To our troops. To future generations?

Joe had his arm around Margot. But his mind was somewhere far away. Atrocities had been committed on both sides, or so he'd heard. But right and wrong in war is never easy to work out. His father had taught him that. He remembered a quote from one of his history books, '*Let him who does not know what war is go to war.*' It could be his turn soon enough.

He watched Margot's minted breath disappear as she whispered to him, 'I'll give you another piece of chewing gum if we can go some place where it's warm. How about Manning House?' Joe knew she would have stayed longer if they'd started singing a few good anti-war songs. *Eve of Destruction* or *Blowing in the Wind* would have been enough.

∗

The amber retreated as Joe tilted his glass away from the light. There were floriated shapes in his Tooth's draught, but it didn't seem to worry him or his fellow students as they celebrated the end of their exams. Joe watched as Margot bobbed and weaved through the hairy horde of revellers at the White Horse. 'I suppose you'd rather another schooner than me at the moment?'

'If it came to the crunch, my love, the odds would be in your favour.' Her closeness and his mildly inebriated state made him even more horny than usual. He'd been living with Margot for almost six months. To say he'd been sleeping with her for that time would give the wrong impression. Mostly they fucked. And yet despite this intense and energetic pastime, he and Margot had attained academic success. Joe had received high distinctions in his final year psych subjects, and Margot had been invited to do an honours year in clinical epidemiology.

One of Joe's psych mentors staggered towards them. Dr Gregory Hopgood MBBS, MD, FRANZCP was a qualified medical psychiatrist who had absconded from his private practice to complete his PhD in post-traumatic stress disorder or PTSD as he referred to it. He lectured in Abnormal Psychology, perhaps Joe's favourite subject. Apart from Dr Hopgood's psychiatric expertise, his other skill was mixing with the student riffraff at the pub. Joe knew him better as *Hops*.

'G'day dear love birds. Congratulations on surviving your respective undergraduate courses. I hear, Joe, you're about to be a *nasho.*' Hops spilled beer down his shirt as he revealed his next venture. 'I'll be in the army myself next month. I've been temporarily seconded into the Royal Australian Army Medical Corps in an advisory capacity. Sounds wonderful doesn't it? Not sure for how long. Apparently, I'm needed over there in Nam. Don't have any ties here, and a bit of overseas travel has always been on my to-do list. *Sic vita est.* Maybe I'll see you over there. Joe, my son, you have talent, whether you recognise it or not. What better material could you have for your master's thesis?'

Hops was about to make his way back to the bar when he thought of something else he wanted to say to Joe. 'I heard you had a mishap with your peace-loving pink VW. If you didn't already know it, the real Che Guevara is now dead. And Che's imitator, our local Batman, is MIA.'

Hops then became distracted by a flicker of light. His attention shifted to observe a moth attacking a burning hot light globe not far from the bar. Joe and Margot looked too. For a while the moth kept missing its mark, then suddenly it sizzled against its target, leaving part of itself behind. It kept on despite all this, searching for another brush with hell. Joe continued to follow the moth's kamikaze mission until he noticed Margot shiver. 'Are you okay my love?'

'It was the reflection of the moth in your eyes, Joe. It freaked me out.'

1969

Dot would lie in her bed with the sheet pulled up over her head. She knew her big brother had sneaked into the room and was waiting to surprise her. Most of the time she couldn't bear the suspense and would give in with streams of uncontrolled laughter. He would then growl and pretend to be a lion or a tyrannosaurus rex. That was back then, when Joe was still at Day Street.

Tonight, he was at Kapooka – its Indigenous meaning is *the place of wind* – where they teach young men to be warriors. Her latest letter from Joe told her about his training – fitness, weapons handling, combat skills, first aid, teamwork, organisational skills. Nothing about how much he missed her. Nothing about the way he felt about the prospect of going to war. She hoped he would slip-up on one of the obstacle courses he wrote about. Maybe he would injure himself just enough to get out of overseas service. She'd seen how clumsy he could be at home.

Dot expected her dad to be proud of him. If he was, he didn't show it. She couldn't understand why he hardly ever spoke about his son anymore. She missed Joe so much already. She remembered one time pleading with him. 'Joe, you won't ever leave me, will you?' Hand on heart he vowed he would be with her always. Not long after that he moved in with Margot. And now he was training for war. Soon he would be at war!

Dot was seventeen when Joe landed in Vietnam.

*

Dot kept thinking of the *Doctor Zhivago* poster she had seen outside the cinema, and tried to imitate the expression on Julie Christie's lips. She was thankful her full lips were good for something at least. And she was happy she could make them look almost identical to those of the movie star. But her nose was different, and she had developed a habit of pinching it, often until it hurt. But every time she let go, it spread back the way it was before. It frustrated her, but she kept at it, hoping it would eventually work.

On one occasion her father caught her in front of the hallway mirror, pinching away as always. 'Are you okay Dot?' He was afraid she'd hurt herself.

'Just squeezing a blackhead dad. Pretty funny joke, hey?' Frank didn't laugh.

Every night before she went to bed, she prayed. She wasn't into blessing all and sundry like she'd done as a child. She prayed for her black hair to be blonde. She prayed she would wake up white, the colour she needed to be to match her mischievous blue eyes. She wanted a thin, delicate nose like Ann Margret. And she wanted Joe to be safely back home with her.

*

'Dad, you know the Furlong's black Labrador. He doesn't realise he's a dog, does he?

Othello was the name on his collar. But the kids called him Otto because it was a better doggy name and easier to say. The family had moved in about a year ago, six houses down the road. Three young children under seven, and a black mutt the size of a Shetland pony. Dot and Winn contributed to his corpulence by giving him leftovers from dinner. Several of the houses in the street did the same.

'He follows the kids around as though he's one of them. They dig in the sandpit. He digs in the sandpit. They jump in the car. He's there already. I wonder what he thinks when they leave him alone tied up outside the church. He's not one of the family all the time, is he?' Dot started to cry and ran down the hallway to her bedroom, spinning nan Winn around and spilling her tea in the process. Winn was about to ask Frank why Dot was so upset, then hesitated when she saw him rereading Joe's letter.

CH 22 – DOT – RESPECT

Tom was pretty sure most of the congregation at the evening Mass weren't following the words of the epistle he was reading. Sometimes he would deliberately skip a few lines to see if the priest or anyone else would notice. So far, no comment. As an occasional celebrant, it was his chance to get noticed. The folk masses at St Mark's were becoming popular with the youth of the parish and, more importantly, the girls. He used to take up the collection plate as well, just to get a better look at the available female talent.

When Communion time came, the choir at the back of the church started singing *What a Wonderful World*. Tom was lost in his own thoughts when an awesome voice passed him on her way to receive the body of Christ. *Christ, it was Dot!* She turned her head away when she realised he was looking at her. He decided on the spot, his rock group needed a lead singer like that. What's more, not only did she have a great voice, she looked a lot like Aretha Franklin. Maybe a little paler. Finally, he heard the line from the priest he was waiting for, 'Go, the Mass has ended.'

'Thanks be to God,' was his reply.

Outside he approached her. 'Hey Dot, how would you like to come to our jam next Saturday? It'll be at the Masonic Hall. An easy walk for you.'

At first, she seemed pleased he'd asked her, but then she played coy. 'I don't know Tom. I have to go to dance class in the morning. Then nan Winn wants me to help her with some cooking in the afternoon. Haven't you got cricket on?'

'Not anymore. I've given that up in favour of becoming a rock star. I really like your voice, Dot. Bring someone if you want. I'm sure the guys won't mind. Let me know what you like to sing, and I'll see if I can make it work in your key.'

'Okay,' she said. She smiled a Julie Christie smile and made her way back down to Day Street, singing as she went, '*Re-re-re-re-re-re-re-re-spect. Just a little bit. Baby, just a little bit…*'

*

The group's name was *Acumen*. Everyone except Bushy, the lead singer, went to the same school. Tom knew Bushy didn't sing that well, but he *did* have access to his father's minivan. He was recruited mainly for transport reasons.

Tom played guitar. Dave Toole was on drums. Pete on bass. And Tony Duffy – better known as Tone Deaf – was on keyboards. Pete brought along Kay as an audience. Tom noticed she liked sitting on his bass speakers a lot of the time. Pete called her KY, but not to her face. Bushy brought along his dad's van. Tom brought along Dot.

While the budding musos tuned up, Dot and Kay got acquainted at the back of the hall. There had been a function there the night before, and the cleaners weren't going to turn up until Monday. Empty beer cans littered the corners of the foyer, but the auditorium itself was relatively uncluttered. The smell of smoke and alcohol was easy enough to get used to.

Dot offered to open some of the windows, but this was vetoed by TD. 'Keeps some of the sound in. We get enough complaints as it is from the neighbouring shops. Gives us more resonance too. You must be Dot.'

'You must be Tone Deaf.' Dot bit her tongue when she said it. The rest of them laughed. TD just shrugged. He'd heard it so often that it went in one ear and out the other.

Tom signalled it was time to start by playing a Hendrix riff. Kay took her position on Pete's speakers. The blue mini she wore clung to her hips like a frightened child. Her hair was long and red and came down to the tip of her bum. Dot's black shoulder-length mop and blue jeans could hardly be in sharper contrast.

It was always a let-down when Kay started to talk. Her words emerged through her nose, not her mouth. Tom cringed when she laughed. He reckoned it was worse than fingernails down a blackboard.

The band started with *Sunshine of Your Love*. Tom showed off by playing Eric Clapton's guitar solo. The others had never heard him play so well. TD then started experimenting with *A Whiter Shade of Pale*, but no-one seemed to know the words except Dot. She took a deep breath and let her voice do the rest. Bushy stopped humming. His mouth hung open so wide it could have held a tambourine. The others joined in as best they could. After a few takes they all agreed they sounded just like *Procol Harum*.

Dot did a Janis Joplin on a *Piece of My Heart*, and that was enough. Tom looked around. 'Has anyone seen Bushy? I think we might have to invest in a van.'

Their first gig together was at the March school dance, doing the warm-up for *Pig Skin*. Dot had never been happier. She turned up with Tom for all the rehearsals. Kay was conspicuously absent.

*

The dance was a flop. Dot was a hit. *Pig Skin* were late. They hassled over their pay. Took long breaks. And over and above the music, there were a couple of all-in brawls that had to be broken up by the police.

The next week, Dot received a shock when she got the results of her recent science test. She had never failed an exam in her life. The euphoria of the last few weeks dissolved as quickly as a pinch of salt in water. Schoolwork mattered more to her than the band. She didn't know how to tell Tom.

She phoned him that night.

'If you're out, I'm out too. I was going to do it before you joined, but then I sort of kept going because of you. How about coming to the uni with me on the weekends? We can study at Fisher Library. But there's a condition.'

'What's that?'

'You have to sing, but just to me. I'll trade my electric guitar for an acoustic. Say yes.'

*

They sat on the front lawn outside Fisher. Tom played. Dot sang. They were lost in their music and their time together. But it was Dot who realised the afternoon was getting away. She still hadn't completed her physics assignment. 'It's study time, Tom. I've got to get back to my quantum mechanics.'

'You mean smoko's over. Back on your heads.'

'What?'

'It's a joke Dot. About people in hell up to their knees in shit, smoking cigars. Then the devil comes along and says …'

'You don't have to tell me any more Tom. Let's go back inside.'

CH 23 – JOE – THE DREAMER

1969

It's good to be away from basic military training. Away from the initial shock of radical haircuts, medicals, and injections by the dozen. After ten weeks of that stuff, I was fit enough to challenge for the Rosehill Guineas. And I would have won too if I hadn't been whisked away for Corps training.

Kapooka never turned out to be what I expected. The physical exercise was hard, but it was straightforward. The food wasn't too bad either. But some of the political palaver they served up to you in the lectures was difficult to stomach. I didn't make waves. No-one did. Which is surprising when you come to think of it. A few of the other uni nashos would have known a lot more about the culture and politics of southeast Asia than many of our instructors.

We were informed about Australia's stance on the war – the official Menzies line – that the takeover of South Vietnam would be a direct military threat to Australia and all the countries of southeast Asia.

Anyway, a lot of my mates, and some of the instructors too, were surprised when I put in my preference for the infantry. Most of the intelligentsia – and I say that light-heartedly – had the catering corps in mind.

At the Jungle Warfare Training Centre at Canungra, we were told we were being sent to Vietnam to kill, to stop the Communists pillaging the land and raping the South Vietnamese women. And if we could stop the nogs over there, our own sisters back home wouldn't have to worry. Most of the blokes in the room seemed to be soaking it all up. Even the priest, called in for the occasion, said it would be permissible to kill for moral reasons. I guess religion and war have been going hand-in-hand for time immemorial. What if we lose? Should I ask the priest? Should we then change our God to the god or gods of the victors? The padre might have flinched at that one.

Many of our instructors had been to Nam and done their tour. They chatted about the heroics and the whores, the excitement and the mateship. And that seemed to have more effect on me than any of the other scripted drivel. Their anecdotes rekindled my own sense of going *over there* and doing whatever it was I had to do.

*

My pre-embarkation leave was divvied up between family, Margot, an empty beach, and a graveyard.

When the time came to go, I flew out with several other reinforcements on the redeye 707 from Mascot. There wasn't much to say that hadn't been said. I kissed and hugged everyone, even dad. Gave a final smile. And they and I were gone. I remember seeing some of the other troops doing their goodbyes too, and I wondered if any of them would come back in a body bag.

I sat next to a thick-set digger on the plane. Around five-ten, thirty, with thick, coarse stubble growing out of every visible pore of his face. Around his eyes too. He smiled to himself, and then to me. 'Joe,' I said.

'The Dreamer,' he said.

I remember learning a poem at school called *The Dreamer* by

Dorothea Mackellar. I can't recall how all of it went, but I finished the first verse in my head while I checked out his hairy smile.

Over the crest of the Hill of Sleep,
Over the plain where the mists lie deep,
Into a country of wondrous things,
Enter we dreaming, and know we're kings.

I asked him, 'Why *The Dreamer*?'

'Because I keep telling myself that everything will turn out all right.'

I remember my dad saying something like that too. I found out he'd been over there before. Then he told me about the first time he landed in Vietnam. And I'm trying to write it down, just the way he told it. Who knows how much of it is true?

'We got to Nam on the Vung Tau Ferry. Some call it the HMAS Sydney. Others refer to it as the big cork in the ocean, because that's what it felt like at sea. Anyway, we got off the converted carrier into American landing barges, the type you see in John Wayne movies. We were a couple of miles off Vung Tau, and we went the rest of the way in full combat gear in these fucking, stinking barges. We were ordered to keep our heads down. You can imagine how we felt. We were shitting ourselves. Our weapons were at the ready. You know, ammunition, the works! The info we got from our CO was brief. *As soon as the front board goes down, hit the beach the best way you can.*'

'Anyway, the leading craft stops. The plank goes down. We hit the beach arse up, tits down. We look up, ready to face a torrent of machine gun fire. And what did we strike? People in black PJs and funny-looking hats selling Coca-Cola, beer, and anything else you want to name. People are riding bikes up and down the beach, and some fuck-arse Yanks and Aussies on R&C are sitting in deck chairs drinking Fosters cheering us on!'

I asked the Dreamer why he'd come back for more. He didn't answer. Maybe he couldn't.

Not long before we landed, he pointed to a strip of lush greenery. 'You wouldn't believe what could be going on underneath all that seeming tranquillity.' I waited for another smile, but on this occasion it didn't come. For the first time I noticed the name on his kit bag. Harry Russell.

It was 11am when we flew into Tan Son Nhut airport, Saigon. Everywhere you looked there was activity. Fighter aircraft, bombers, helicopters. South Vietnamese troops, all armed, wandering around seemingly with no destination in mind. There was this god-almighty stink that pervaded everything. And there they were … body bags! I looked at the Dreamer. He had an idea what I was thinking.

'You'll get used to it. Or not.'

They lined us up on the tarmac and brought out lunch for us. Most of us played around with it for a while, then threw it in the bin. The humidity was unbearable. We were stuffed after the long flight anyway. Then we got loaded onto a bus. As it pulled away, I looked back at the previously invisible airport workers swarming around the garbage bins. Getting stuck into our partly eaten pieces of fruit and mangled morsels of sandwich.

So, I was finally here. And I was already scared beyond belief. The feeling wasn't helped by the reinforced wire mesh that covered all the windows of the bus. I looked through the mesh. An old man was having a shit at the side of the road. I looked again. A teenage girl carrying a baby spat at us as our bus went by.

CH 24 – JOE – FOUR MAN HOOCH

1969

When we got to Nui Dat, we were met by the platoon commander and assigned to our respective hoochies.

The four-man tent I was directed to had sandbags and corrugated iron packed around it for protection against mortar attacks. There was hardly anything else inside, except for some makeshift flooring, a locker, a folding table, and chairs. And three men who sat there inspecting me. All were drinking beer. In fact, by the look of the pile of empty cans, they must have been drinking beer for quite a while. Just the same, none of them seemed to be in the slightest bit pissed.

Partly hidden by the shade, the biggest of the three directed me with a twist of his head. 'Put your kitbag down there, mate. That used to be Boris' spot. He copped one in the arse and now he's back in Canberra. Back in Aussie heaven.' There was something about the way he said a/rrr/se that took me back to my uni days in linguistics. When he stood up and moved from the corner of the tent, I knew what it was. He was an Indigenous Aussie like my sis, with a thick Adelaidean rhotic '/r/' sound. 'My name's Norm, but they call me Bluey or Blue because of the colour of my hai/rrr/.' His hair was orange red.

'Glad to meet you.' Bluey held out his hand, looking carefully at my response. When I took it with a certain fervour, the others seemed to relax. Apparently, I had passed some preordained test. 'There are too many nogs around here to worry about the odd boong,' he chuckled. 'My full name is Norman Lindsay. Just like the other Aussie legend. Artist, writer, fighter. Me.' He eyed my look of disbelief. 'It really is my name. I kid you not. My dad was a fan.' His grin was friendly enough, but at the same time, at least for me, it was also a touch intimidating.

The two other occupants of the hooch eased themselves out of their fold-down chairs and introduced themselves.

The short one had the voice of a radio announcer. Deep, with a slight European intonation. His Scottish cap, complete with red pom-pom, made him look a little taller than what he actually was. I think he was probably happy with this effect. And he wore a tartan kilt too, with a matching sporran. 'My name is Alberto Lombardino. Just call me *Scotty*. Everyone else in this bog hole does. The kilt and the other Caledonian odds and ends mask my true Sicilian ancestry. As the others will tell you, I am a *paranza corta* master of the folding stiletto, but I also play the Great Highland bagpipes to an alacritous but mixed reception. Traditionalists sometimes find it confusing when they see me holding the bag under my right arm. But when I play the pipes, the sound of the skirl is amazing. I can teach you anything you want to know about the art of the assassin, but don't ask me how to play the bagpipes. I play them my own way, like no-one else can.'

'Yeah, like no-one else ever should,' the remaining digger mumbled. The quietest of the three was around five-eleven. My height. Past that, he was a mixture of gristle and muscle. He was prematurely bald, which he made up for by the thick tangle of hair on his chest. Through the throng of hair, a large tattoo was discernible in the form of a giant 'S'. I'm *Superman* to my friends, and Corporal Kenneth Campbell to my platoon commander. My name's more Scottish than this bagpipe of shite – pointing to Scotty – but I don't have his flair for the highland fashion. You can borrow any of my Superman comics for ten cents a time, or my science fiction books for double that. Boris, the nasho you are replacing, borrowed *Kingdom Come,* and still hasn't returned it to me. I'll chase him up on that issue when I get back to Canberra. Being medevacked out isn't a good enough excuse as far as that goes. By the way, all three of us are regulars. Maybe we'll teach you a few tricks to help you get back home in one piece.'

'Tell us about yourself,' came Scotty's booming voice. 'We know you are a Sydneysider with the good Irish-Catholic name of Keneally. And we already know you are a green-as-pesto nasho too. What else?'

I thought about what I should say, and what I shouldn't say. 'My dad's an ex-army engineer. POW under the Japs.' I glanced at Blue. 'My adopted sis is First Nations too.' No response so far. I kept thinking. 'I have a degree in psych. And …'

'That's enough for us now mate. We'll get to know you more in good time. But we need to give you a proper name, don't we? Wait a sec.'

A minute later Bluey emerged from the three-man huddle with a serious look on his face. 'After conferring with my colleagues, we have come to a decision. You are *Shrink* from now on. Pretty obvious, is it not?'

Fair enough, I thought. It could have been a lot worse.

Scotty added, 'You're in deep shit, Shrink. This place is a bugger to live through as it is without having to analyse it as well.'

CH 25 – JOE – INCOMING

Letters to my family and Margot aren't going to be a good enough of an outlet for my thoughts. What kind of things can you tell them in all this confusion? Hopefully, I'll be able to keep the flow of innocuous mail going, mainly as a means of reassuring them I'm okay. That I'm still alive. More importantly, a constant flow from my end ensures I get a healthy flow of letters back. One of my first letters was entitled *Christmas at the Dat*. After that one they sent me a tape with all of them singing *Crimson and Clover* over and over. Over and over. I forgot how well Dot could sing. Margot wasn't bad either.

The Dreamer reckons he read dozens of Golden Books to his son during his first tour back in '66. His wife kept sending him books and blank tapes. Tom and Jerry, Peter Pan, 101 Dalmatians, you name it. He kept laying the stories down and sending the tapes back.

I ask myself: why has this seemingly normal family man come back to this stink hole?

*

I'm starting to get used to the ins and outs of the artillery already. Not so long ago I treated every boom as an incoming mortar. Now I'm more scared of what the others do in their sleep. Superman and

Bluey are already getting to the end of their tours. Scotty still has a while to go on this, his second one. His previous time here was in '67. From what I can gather, his marriage broke up not long after he got back. That doesn't seem to worry him much anymore, but something does. His current tour is only a couple of months old, but he keeps waking up in these sweats, screaming something about bamboo pickers, body counts, kids. Superman does it too.

The mossies among other things here are pretty bad, although I've been told they could be a lot worse if it wasn't for the constant spraying. The planes fly over regularly, bombing the jungle and us with various insecticides. They tell us these so-called Rainbow Herbicides stop the vegetation from hiding the nogs. It's one of our familiar morning smells.

The Dreamer came around yesterday to make sure the other blokes were treating me all right. His hooch is on the other side of the 1ATF camp. He asked me if I've been marking off my calendar. I pulled it out from under my notes and showed him the neat red crosses, one next to the other. One and a half rows duly completed. 'Ten days already. Hey Shrink, you're a real veteran.' He'd already picked up my new name. 'By the way, I hear we're going in-country in a few days.'

The Australian Forces Radio was playing *'Born to be Wild'* as he spoke. And just as they were singing *'Fire all of your guns at once, and ...'* Scotty comes in and spoils the end of the song.

'My fellow ATF diggers, did you hear the one about the Irish VC who replanted an Aussie mine? He kept jumped up and down on it to be sure, to be sure it still worked.'

'No. What happened? Why did he do that? It doesn't make sense.' Superman was egging Scotty on.

'He blew himself up dickhead. That's the joke. Don't you get it? He was an Irish nog.'

We were all laughing. Scotty realised the joke had been played back on him. He took it in good humour. 'I'll get back at you bastards, just you wait!' Then he stopped still and held up his hand. 'Sshhh … Incoming! Incoming!' The faraway sound of pop, pop, pop was soon accompanied by an explosion, then another. We scampered to the sandbags for protection.

The attack only lasted a minute or so, but the 82mm mortars killed one of the cooks, wounded two others, and wrecked a jeep. The only casualty in our hoochie group was Superman who crunched his balls as he leapt out of his bunk.

'Ah fuck, fuck, fuck, fuck …' was all Superman could contribute while he rolled around on the ground in agony.

Scotty thought his antics were a scream.

CH 26 – JOE – JUMPING JACK FLASH

I'll never get used to these conditions. Rashes, trench foot, crotch rot, leeches – at least the enemy had to put up with the same things. Oodles of snakes and spiders were surpassed only by the bites they inflicted. And the NVA and VC themselves.

Most of the guys had been in-country before. This was my first. I was trying hard not to act like a newbie. Our group's counter-insurgency tactics meant we were going to be doing these kinds of patrols a lot of the time. Scotty, Blue, and Superman had given me the drill about the possibility of Viet Cong booby traps. The area we were in had lots of tall grass too, and things like punji spikes, tripwires, and cartridge traps were incredibly difficult to detect.

I was thinking I was doing okay when I stubbed my foot on a piece of bamboo. It was neatly protruding through the surface of the ground. Maybe too neatly. I'd seen these things at Corps training in Canungra. I fell back from the spot and jumped as far away as I could. Nothing happened.

Bluey saw me dive and alerted the others in case of ambush. Again, nothing.

I found out later another five of these 'toe-poppers' had been discovered in the same zone. Thankfully, none had been set off by an ill-fated footfall. Each one consisted of a single round of ammo set into a piece of bamboo that had been lowered into a hole in the ground. At the bottom of the bamboo was a board and a nail. Pressure turned the nail into a firing pin. I had been lucky. I still had my toes.

*

I write this from Vungers while on unplanned R&C.

Two weeks after I stubbed my foot on a 'toe-popper' one of our platoon planted his boot on something much bigger. An M16 mine has no friends. The 'jumping jack' leapt into the air, spraying shrapnel in all directions. I must have been a good thirty metres from the blast, but I went down like a sack of spuds. Once I got myself together, I instinctively made my way to where the blast came from. The sound of a thousand cicadas was ringing in my ears.

Up until that moment, I had never seen a dead person. I brushed past the remains of what must have been the unfortunate trooper that detonated the mine. Then I got to the Dreamer not far away. Harry's face was untouched. He had this puzzled, surprised expression frozen onto it. The rest of him was a mangled mess of bloodied flesh and bone.

I stared down into the Dreamer's unresponsive eyes. Blood dripped into them. My blood.

*

I woke up to the beating drums of an Iroquois rotor. Strapped next to me inside the medivac chopper was Scotty. The medic was trying to stem the flow of blood from my head while Scotty yelled the punchline of a joke at him. Scotty's leg was already bandaged. The wrapping around my head was getting redone.

The medic was shouting to my mafioso-come-highlander friend to

95

shut up while he attended to my partially detached ear. I recognised
Steve Watson's desperate and unsuccessful cries from times gone by.
A time when a man of the cloth was brutally beating the shit out of
his son, while claiming he was doing it out of love.

'Wotto!' I sobbed.

'Joe?'

Scotty and I were transported to the Base Hospital at Vung Tau
where we spent the next couple of weeks getting patched up. I had
the top half of my ear sown back on under a local anaesthetic that
didn't work. Scotty had his leg shaved and stitched. Given the size
of the M16 blast, our platoon didn't suffer as badly as we might have
if we hadn't been widely dispersed. Two dead. Four wounded. I will
never forget the Dreamer's face for the rest of my life.

*

Wotto came to see me a couple of times while I was recovering, but
he never stayed long enough for me to ask him any questions about
himself and his family. Maybe I'm not thinking too straight at the
moment anyway. I keep getting lots of headaches and dizzy spells too.
I'm hoping that most of this weird head-fog is a temporary left-over
from the blast. Scotty on the other hand has been up and about since
day four. Somehow, he must have got his hands on some speed. He
can't stay still. He wants to get back to the hooch, his kilt, and his
pipes. He's such a strange, likable, but unpredictable character that
still screams in his sleep, even here.

Finally, after two weeks of Vunger's best and worst cuisine, one
of the doctors came around and told us to piss off. With a smile on
his dial, he called us a pair of malingerers and ordered us back to the
Dat with his commanding officer's blessings. And then he says to me,

'By the way, Dr Hopgood sends his best. Says he's looking forward to reading your master's thesis one day.'

CH 27 – JOE – THE MAN IN THE HIGH CASTLE

'Now you've returned to our palace, Shrink, you need to get stuck into some of this stuff.' The man with the S-shaped tattoo on his chest gave a nod to the stack of science fiction novels next to his bunk. 'It's made me into the astute, truth-seeker I am today. A learned gent like you needs more than a comic.' Superman threw me a book. Its name was *The Man in the High Castle* by Philip K. Dick.

I told him I wasn't into science fiction that much because it was too far removed from reality. He inclined his head and laughed. 'Like fucking hell it isn't real. *1984* used to be called SF until it wasn't. The book Philip Dick wrote will blow your academic brain away.' He sat down on his chair and continued in a very thoughtful manner. 'Most things lack reality in some form or other. Life is fiction as soon as it's written down. What's important depends on whether or not it has meaning for you.'

I read Dick's novel in a couple of sittings. It's the story of a world like our own, but in this one Germany and Japan won World War 2. In the book, the man in the high castle is a novelist who writes about an alternative world where Germany and Japan lost. The alternative world in which the allied powers won is also a world with its own kind of repression. And the crazy thing is, the characters in the story begin to realise they are part of the fiction too.

I started wondering if our own idea of victory in Vietnam is also fiction. And the enemy we're fighting against has already won.

*

We've just been told by the platoon commander that the Dreamer's wife took her own life after she heard about his death. Apparently, their only son drowned a few months before Harry returned for his second tour. He once told me, 'Everything will turn out all right.' But I now remember the whole of the last verse of Dorothea Mackellar's poem. *'Everything will turn out all right'* but only if the dreamer never wakes.

> *Murmur or roar as it may, the stream*
> *Laughs to the youngster who dreams his dream.*
> *Leave him alone till his fool's heart breaks:*
> *Dreams all are real till the dreamer wakes!*

CH 28 – JOE – A LIFELESS HAND

I got my first kill today. Scotty keeps patting me on the back and telling me I'm no longer a virgin soldier. It's an episode in my life I would rather forget.

Our platoon had several contacts over the past two or three weeks. And we were pretty sure we'd killed a few of them, but we could never find any bodies. This time I was following a blood trail when I came across a fresh dig. I was just about to check it out when a group of VC made their way through a small clearing.

They didn't see us at first. Then there was firing all around the place. There were four them. Two carked it straight away. The other two broke free and started running in my direction. They didn't have a clue I was there. I just sighted them and kept firing. That was it. One of them went down as though his power pack had been switched off. The other one spun around like a breakdancer, then kept coming at me even though he'd been hit several times. I continued to fire until finally the top of his head broke free.

Everything suddenly went quiet. Stupidly, I sat down on the mound of dirt I was going to check and got goosed by a lifeless hand that was protruding through the soil.

'Four plus this one makes five. Not bad for a day's work.' I looked up as Scotty pulled out his knife and souvenired the ears off my breakdancer. 'Good price for these on the black,' he murmured.

Bluey called me over. 'This one's not dead, Shrink. He's yours.'

I came to the one I'd hit first. He looked about fourteen and would have weighed seven stone dripping wet. He lay there letting out a terrible, unnatural sound that I can best describe as a mucous-filled snort every time he exhaled. He was too bad to move. I'd stitched him across his belly and chest, and his small upper body was gaping like an unzipped tote bag.

He knew I was the one that shot him by the way he singled me out with his eyes. His stare wasn't one of vengeance or of pain. Without words he asked me to help him die. I started to bend down to take his hand when Bluey pulled me away. Superman finished him off with a single shot. We dragged him over and heaped him with the others for burial.

'Accommodation for five, sir,' I heard from one of our party. 'Four very fresh, one slightly off.'

CH 29 – JOE – REST & CONVALESCENCE

On average, we'd go down to Vungers once a month for R&C. All of us would squash into the back of a truck, arms and legs this way and that, and we'd rattle down the road for twenty or thirty klicks, stopping every now and then to throw someone back in the truck after they'd fallen out.

It's got to be one of the most dangerous things I've done since I've been here.

Blue and I gravitated to the same bar this time. 'What've you got planned, Shrink? Maybe freshen up *Percy* with one of the bargirls?'

He must have seen me wince, because he slapped me on the back and gave me another option. 'I know just the place for a couple of battle-weary, bronzed Aussies.' He flashed a blinding smile and led me down to the beach.

On the way we passed a couple of black GIs. 'You know it really pisses me off when all these dudes call me *brother* and start jive talkin' as though I'd understand what they're saying. Next time I'll answer them back in *Kaurna*.'

He looked at my blank face. 'The language of the Adelaide Plains people. My people mate. Abo talk. Maybe I'll get a Featherfoot to *sing* them away.' I didn't follow him again. 'Doesn't your sister teach you anything?'

We walked along the sand for a few minutes, then headed towards a little restaurant on the beach front. Bluey said it was a favourite hangout of his. 'I wouldn't trust Scotty in this place, but Superman's been here with me a couple of times. Both those guys will be ratshit after the sniffing and gambling they'll be doing tonight.'

Blue took me down the side of the place and around to the back. He knocked twice, then three times. A young Vietnamese boy in his mid-teens answered the door. 'Norman! You come in.'

To me the boy looked like VC, so I backed off a few steps until I could plainly see that Blue knew where he was going. A movement of his hand was all I needed, and I was in there after him.

I heard the youth whisper to Blue, 'You tell your friend about *dust of life*?'

'*Dust*' … I was thinking powder – cocaine or heroin. I couldn't have been further from the truth.

Inside the large room there were a dozen or so children – babies, toddlers. Many of them were obviously of mixed parentage: Vietnamese-Black American, Vietnamese-White American, maybe a few with a touch of Aussie. Their mothers were having their hair done for the night shift.

Blue turned to me and shrugged his shoulders. 'It's all business, Shrink. Ultimately, the kids always end up the losers.'

'That friend of yours from when you were kids – Wotto the dust-off man – you know he's a compulsive thief?' I shook my head in disbelief. 'He's also a saint! He has ways of finding toys and writing materials for the local orphanage. Somehow, he even gets drugs and medical supplies to where they're needed most. He's more than a saint. He's a good person. Not all saints are.'

We were taken upstairs to a private table, and each given a can of XXXX. Then we had the greatest feast I've ever had in my life. I told Bluey he was a man of surprises. 'I do my best,' was his reply. 'Of course, it'll cost you six times the going rate for the food.'

I told him it was worth it. 'All in a good cause.'

Bluey paid the ultimate price for our tête-à-tête – the story of my life. He seemed all-ears when I spoke about my sister Dot. And in a strange way, I was jealous of his connection by kinship with her.

*

The next day we caught up with Scotty and Superman. They'd been fleeced by an eight-year-old kid before they even had a chance to finish their first doobie. So to get to the game they started calling in a few old debts – some legit, some not. It ended up in a pub brawl that both apparently enjoyed. For the next two nights, neither of them woke me up with their screaming or moaning. I didn't share their silence. The earthquakes and the ear-piercing cicadas had returned.

*

Bluey is an interesting sort of bloke. He's the youngest of six – two boys, four girls. His family still live out of Adelaide, where his father used to be a stockman, now turned storeman and packer.

'I ran away to Sydney when I was eighteen to escape my family's web. Expectations about how I should be. How my folks and the locals wanted me to be.' Blue joined the army soon afterwards and was a regular for five years before he was sent to Vietnam.

I'll be sorry to see Bluey and Superman go, but the end of their tours is approaching. They're becoming extra cautious these days, too cautious maybe. I wish I could join them on the trip home, but I still have more time here. Besides, Scotty and I need to break in some new blood in the hooch.

Blue isn't so sure about what he'll do or where he'll go when he gets back. He's even thought of staying on in the army for a couple more years, then go bush.

Superman reckons he might do a trade – sparky, chippie or dunny diver – or even start a removals business. He's already given heaps of his science fiction books to me, and what's left, he's taking home for his private library. He reckons they'll fill out the shelves in his study so Dostoyevsky, Camus, and Kafka don't fall over. Not like I'm starting to do myself. I've become an erratic ground-sitter until the world decides to stop moving. The buzzing in my head is driving me crazy.

CH 30 – JOE – FRONT TOWARDS ENEMY

1970

I've changed. Things have changed. How can I put this?

We came out of the bush and started plodding along an old dirt road.

'Seven days to go. Seven days to go.' Superman's singing was irritating. And out-of-tune too. But it broke the monotony, so what can I say? We hadn't had any contacts the entire week. Not that anyone really minded.

Up ahead, about two hundred metres or so, we spotted some villagers moving in the same direction we were. Scotty thought it'd be worthwhile to check them out. We broke into a trot and got halfway when … BOOM! We hit the dirt. We knew it was the sound of a Claymore. But the thing is, a Claymore mine is directional. It had obviously been pointing the wrong way when some misinformed nog detonated it. If the VC want to use our own ammo against us, they should also know a smattering of English first. The print on the device says it all. FRONT TOWARDS ENEMY means *front towards enemy*! If you get it wrong you get shredded, like the trees on the other side of the road. And probably the nogs that set it up.

None of us were even the slightest bit hurt. We waited for enemy fire. None came. We gave off a few rounds into the scrub. Nothing. Then we saw what looked like two VC closing in on us, running down the middle of the road.

We were about to fire on them when Scotty screams out, 'Wait! Don't fire.' They kept getting closer. Again, 'Hold your fire!' They were close enough now to see it was two women. One pretty old. The other just pretty. Scotty keeps on, but with all the screaming the only thing Superman seems to have heard is '… fire!'

He stands up with his Armalite. 'What if there's a grenade in the …' The rest of what he shouted was drowned out by automatic fire that sliced the two women to pieces.

When we got to them, the first thing we did was go through their baskets. Fruit and vegetables. Then we searched the mutilated bodies. No weapons.

Scotty glanced at me fleetingly before thrusting a grenade into the middle of one of the baskets. 'Fuck! Look at this,' indicating the grenade. The platoon commander didn't need to be told any more. He already knew.

Scotty was a mass of sweat. He started to take out his knife, then stopped. 'Same thing happened to me in '67. You just don't have a clue who's going to try to kill you next. We were lucky today on both counts. Let's bury them and get out of here.' But then Superman pulls out his knife and finishes what Scotty was about to do.

On the way back to camp, I kept thinking about one of books Superman gave me. It was by a guy named Ballard. The book was called *The Crystal World*. In the book there is some kind of mysterious force that starts crystallising the jungle and all the things inside it – the beautiful and the misshapen, the good and the bad, the sane and the mad, the living and the dead. It didn't matter who or what. Everything and everyone eventually turned into the same thing. It unsettled me. Made me think about a lot of things. I sent it off to Wotto. He's turned out to be a bit of a reader and a poet. And I wondered if

Ballard's book would have the same effect on him.

*

Not long after the Claymore incident, I had another one of my 'turns'. At first, I had roaring in one of my ears. The not-so-pretty one. Then the world started to spin, and I just dropped to the ground.

I write this entry from Vung Tau Base Hospital. I'm here again. I feel fine now. And I wonder if I'm not going through some kind of an anxiety thing. The doctors at first thought I had all the symptoms of a condition known as Ménière's Disease. But given my history of blast trauma and loss of hearing, they think it might be something else. And the cicadas! They're inside my head all the time now. It looks like I'll be going back to Oz with Bluey and Superman after all.

CH 31 – JOE – DRIFTING IN THE VOID

1970

I looked out the window. It was Saigon. Hours later, it was Sydney.

Bluey and Superman were my flight buddies. They got through stacks of Foster's Lager on the way. For them, Nam was done. But not for me. At least not yet. Once I'm sorted, I'll be back. Back with Scotty, Wotto, and Hops – and the newbies they'll be sending us. But first I need to rejig myself from being *Drop Joe* to *Shrink* again.

*

We landed at Kingsford Smith at 22:00, May 6th. The new International Terminal had just been opened and everything was palatial, at least compared to the way it was when we left. It would have been nice to think they'd done all the improvements just for us. But that was quickly sent packing by what followed.

Customs gave us a really hard time, looking for drugs and souvenirs. We didn't expect that. Maybe a brass band, not the third degree. At least we didn't get a cavity search. They probably thought we had dysentery and didn't want to take the chance.

Out of Customs, we were confronted by a mob of protesters, waving placards in front of our faces. Calling us murderers of women and children.

Superman didn't hang around for any of that crap, and sprinted off with a couple of mates to catch a chartered connecting flight to his hometown of Canberra. We hardly had time to say good-bye. 'Catch up with you.' His voice disappeared into the chant of the hecklers.

War crimes! War crimes! Melting cheese and Vietnamese!

I looked in vain for anyone with a kind, familiar face. I went into the men's room and slammed the cubicle door shut. Bluey was lost in all the confusion. I sat there for half an hour reading one of Superman's books about revenge.

The guy in the book is Gulliver Foyle. He's in a wrecked spaceship drifting in the void when he sees another vessel. It ignores his signs of distress, and simply passes him by. He changes from an ordinary, peace-abiding man into a man seeking revenge. *The Stars My Destination* is the name of the book. Through a series of adventures and misadventures, Gully Foyle kills the crew of the other spaceship one-by-one, and finally puts an end to all war by giving everyone a secret explosive – in effect, a loaded gun. He says, 'I've handed life and death back to the people who do the living and the dying.'

By the time I came out into the waiting area, all the protesters had gone. Bluey was sitting there patiently, reading a newspaper. 'I knew you'd come out eventually. I'm guessing it must have been the food on the plane. Come to think of it, it did taste a bit funny.'

He made me smile, like the Dreamer made me smile. I was glad he was home for good.

'Let's go out and catch a cab.' As soon as Bluey and I got through the doors, I spotted Venus waiting in the parking area. She was empty, but I knew at least Margot was somewhere nearby. I did an about-turn and raced back into the terminal. Blue followed. There they were – Margot, Dot, and dad – bewildered among the torn pieces of placard. They hadn't seen me yet.

CH 32 – JOE – THE BIG SQUEEZE

1970

It turns out it hadn't been easy for Margot to find a parking spot for the beetle, but eventually she'd been lucky enough to get one right near airport arrivals just as some of the protesters were pulling out.

By the time she, Dot, and dad made it inside the terminal it was a hotch-potch of mangled anti-war posters that were quickly disappearing as an army of cleaning staff started erasing evidence of the recent pandemonium. Margot must have been desperate – thinking she'd been too late to meet me. To top it all off, earlier on they'd been given a bum steer by one of the protesters who was only too happy to point them in the wrong direction for the troop arrivals.

I shouted out to them until I was blue in the face, but my voice could barely be heard above the sound of the vacuum cleaners and polishers. Dot saw me first and came over, tears streaming down her face. She just hugged me. The others got to me seconds later.

I greeted dad with a 'Hi, I'm home.' At first, he extended his hand in the manner of a gentleman's greeting, then he grasped my neck and gave me the equivalent of a champion wrestler's bear hug. Margot's embrace was a little more delicate, mingled with a big, wet kiss.

Bluey had been forgotten in all the confusion. I looked around and noticed he'd dragged up both kitbags and gently placed them nearby. He gave me a sheepish smile and said, 'I'll be off now.'

I wasn't as timid in my reply. 'You take one step away from us, Blue, and you're history!'

Back came his comment, turning to my dad. 'Do you see what the army has done to your son Mr Keneally? He's bossy. Officer material.' Bluey obviously remembered that my father had been an officer during World War 2. Dad chuckled, then gave him a firm handshake.

I did the other introductions. 'This handsome gent is known as Bluey or Blue. His other name is Norman.'

My dad smiled. 'We know all about you, Bluey, from Joe's letters.'

'Pleased to meet you, Mr Keneally.'

'This is my girlfriend, Margot.' Blue gave a knowing nod.

'And this is my brainy little sister, Dot, who isn't so little anymore.'

Blue hesitated and started to dip his hat before he remembered he'd already taken it off. 'Glad to meet you, Dorothy.'

'Charmed, Mr Norman?'

'Lindsay.' Dot extended her hand for a shake, but Bluey gently took it and kissed it in a most chivalrous manner, occasioning a smile and a blush.

Without thinking about the limited space inside Venus I said something like, 'We'll give you a lift to the city Blue. Where are you going?'

'It's okay Joe. I'll get a cab.'

'Cut it out Blue. Where are you off to?'

'Surry Hills mate. I'll be staying with some friends for a while until I work out what I'm doing with my leave.'

'Done.'

We all laughed when two kitbags, the driver, and four passengers were lined up next to the VW beetle. I remember the squeeze in the back seat as one of the best parts of my welcome home.

Norm tumbled out of the car once we got to Surry Hills. It reminded me of the R&C trips we did to Vung Tau. I walked him to the door of the run-down semi. We said our goodbyes as well as the situation allowed, but Blue in the end couldn't contain himself. I was about to get back in the car when I heard a raucous shout, 'Keep your head down Shrink. And take good care of that little sister of yours. She'll be Prime Minister one day.'

I looked around at my digger mate and yelled back at him, almost as loud, 'And you, Mr Norman Lindsay, are a serious bullshit artist!'

Venus backfired her farewell. Bluey hit the ground instinctively.

CH 33 – MARGOT – SOULMATE

1970

The first thing that struck Winn was his lean appearance. Joe had been a stone heavier when he left Sydney six or so months ago. She also noticed he'd grown his sandy hair longer, combing it in a way that partially covered his right ear. Later that night she took a closer look at the lumpy scar surrounding the misshapen rim and lobe. Joe noticed Winn staring at him and joked that some of his army mates tried to souvenir it while he was asleep on picket. Winn didn't think his wisecrack was funny at all. In her opinion his sense of humour had deteriorated a great deal.

Margot on the other hand saw Joe in a different light. As far as she was aware, she was the only one back home he'd told about the 'toe-popper', or about what happened to his friend the Dreamer. Her former boyish lover had been remodelled into what some would call a warrior, but she would call her consummate man, her life-long soulmate. She prayed he would never have to return to Vietnam.

*

For Joe, breakfast the next morning was like the old days, with Winn trying her best to spoil him. Corn flakes and orange juice, bacon and eggs, toast and jam, and a hot cup of tea. He wondered if he was in paradise.

The roaring in his head hit him suddenly. He had just enough time to put the cup back on the table before falling to the floor.

*

Over the next few weeks, Joe was in and out of various hospitals and private medical clinics. First the army doctors prodded and poked. Then the Macquarie Street specialists had their turn. Radiologists, neurologists, otolaryngologists all searching for a cause and cure for his headaches, his vertigo, and his hearing problems.

Their findings indicated that shrapnel from the 'jumping jack' mine had not only damaged the cartilage and skin of his external ear, it had also ruptured his eardrum and dislocated the tiny ossicles or hearing bones in his middle ear. The latter was the main cause of his vertigo, and the ENT surgeon was confident it could all be put right. Not only that, the specialist informed Joe he would carry out some plastic reshaping of the ear and surrounding tissue at the same time. Joe was happy about that. He thought his hair looked better short anyway.

Surgery was performed early July. By the end of August, a rejuvenated Joe was playing footy again in the park. This time he only had a 'drop attack' when he got his legs taken out from under him by a bootlace tackle. At the beginning of September, he was reviewed by the army doctors and deemed fit to return to Vietnam at the end of the year.

When the news reached Margot, she was so distraught she told Winn the story of the moth at the White Horse Inn. And how she imagined it to be Joe, forever attracted to his own private hell. Her prayers to prevent him going back to war seemed destined to remain unanswered.

CH 34 – DOT – TOP MARKS

Every time the automatic sliding doors of Fisher Library opened, the draft scattered the Moratorium posters and pamphlets into an intensifying anarchistic pattern.

STOP THE WAR.

WITHDRAW ALL TROOPS.

ABOLISH CONSCRIPTION.

NOT WITH MY SON YOU DON'T.

STOP WORK TO STOP THE WAR.

BRING TROOPS HOME NOW.

*

Tom didn't know much about the political issues surrounding the war in Vietnam. Even Dot's understanding of what was going on was fuelled more by what she saw on television than what Joe told her in his sketchy letters from Nui Dat. But she was well aware that the spirit of protest spreading through society had escalated, and that public opinion was now influencing the way the war was being fought. She also knew that the anti-war movement was having an impact on the well-being of the returning troops, including Joe. She remembered the accusations of the airport protesters – the daily news headlines, photos, video footage. And she wondered how her beautiful brother was going to deal with the inevitability of returning to war.

*

'Hey Dot, are you going to the rally on the 18th?'

'You must be kidding, Tom. What would Joe think? I couldn't do that to him. Anyway, it's just before my maths assignment is due. And then I've got that deadline on the *Voss* essay.'

'I understand you want to support Joe and be with him whenever you can, especially now. But you have to realise it's not the end of the world if you don't top the class in every subject!'

'Yes it is. I want to do medicine at Sydney Uni, and I've got to get top marks for that.'

'Med's not for me, Dot. You get called out at night. Patients die on you. And looking at those disintegrating bodies all day can't be pleasant. How could you think of doing it?'

'So what turns you on then, Tom? Have you decided how the world will be graced by your considerable talents?'

'Well, now you mention it, and since I've given the idea of being a rock star the arse, I think I'll become either a dentist or the world's greatest lover, or both.'

*

Dot tried to put the prospect of Joe returning to Vietnam out of her mind. But every time she thought of him, she was reminded of what was about to happen. Schoolwork and even Tom became unimportant. It would be a dream come true if her brother didn't have to go back. She just wanted him to stay with her and be the same old Joe again.

CH 35 – JOE – THE NAKED SOLDIER

I got up early this morning, put on some of my old civilian clothes, left a note, and went to catch a bus into the city.

I breathed in the air. City air. Sydney air. Spring air. It was so different from Nui Dat air. The planes that flew overhead on their way to Mascot weren't spraying anything on me either.

On my way down Day Street, I came across Otto the black Labrador. Or perhaps I should say, he came across me. He was already on his morning food-gathering rounds. He wagged his tail until his whole body began to shake. He slobbered over my hand, hoping I had a treat. I told him he was getting fatter. He didn't seem to care.

Just before I reached the bus stop, I saw Kay, one of Dot's friends. She was always on the lookout for a man. I braced for her welcome, but she ignored me completely. Two buses on route to the city arrived together. She made sure she didn't take the one I did. Kay had never been short of a word and a flick of her hair in the old days. Maybe she's tagged me as a murderer. I wouldn't be surprised.

The bus took me down Victoria Road, through Rozelle and Pyrmont, and then on to the CBD. The colours, even in September, were welcome relief from the constant blacks and greens of Vietnam.

I got out in Market Street and walked along to the Town Hall. There in front of me was a stylised image of an Australian soldier holding a Vietnamese child by the feet, ready to lop its head off in front of its mother. Still further on, painted along a wall, were the words, '*Hitler burned Jews, we burn Asians.*'

The tension was building up inside me, the way I get just before I squeeze the trigger. Only this time I didn't know what I was aiming at.

I saw a couple of R&R Yanks stumbling along George Street. They must have been on the piss all night. I suspect they had trouble even seeing the ground in front of them, let alone the anti-war propaganda. But if they realised what all the placards and graffiti were saying, they would have diced their uniforms in favour of what I had on.

Hyde Park returned some of my composure. I strolled down the tree-lined path to the ANZAC War Memorial. Its *art deco* setbacks and buttresses were punctuated on each side by a huge window of yellow stained glass. Inside was the sculpture of a naked soldier. Dead. He was held aloft on his shield by three female figures representing his mother, his sister, and his wife. I stood there for another half hour and cried.

Later on, I made my way down to Chinatown. The whole place was unsettling. Some of the laneways reminded me of Saigon. It was as though a little piece of Asia had been implanted into an otherwise western labyrinth. Same as what's going on in my brain at the moment.

Having reached Surry Hills, I had this irresistible urge to go and poke my nose in on Bluey. I plodded on as though I was on patrol, one foot in front of the other. Searching for where we dropped him off from the airport. I couldn't find it. So many of the semis looked the same. I must have knocked on a dozen doors. I gave up. Maybe Blue just walked around the corner after we took off. Maybe he got into a taxi and went somewhere else. There's a chance I'll never find out.

I trotted back to Central Station, sweating under the thick jumper I was wearing. The heat made me feel better. I hopped onto a train, then walked to my next rendezvous – St Patrick's Catholic Cemetery, North Parramatta. The place hadn't changed that much. I took it all in.

Alice Enez Keneally 1926-1950. Loving wife of Francis. Devoted Mother of Joseph. Gone too soon. Until we meet again.

Man is made by his beliefs. As he believes, so he is.

CH 36 – MARGOT – LIVING WITH ANOTHER MAN

1970

Joe got back from his jaunt around the CBD and St Patrick's by mid-afternoon. Greeted by Winn, he kissed her on the cheek and sat out on the veranda with a can of beer and a notebook.

Dot arrived home an hour or so later, and the two of them squeezed together on the one-and-a-half seater chatting about the important things in Dot's life – music, schoolwork, and Tom. A backfire from Venus interrupted the exchange. Joe jumped, but not as far as Bluey did after his night-time ride from the airport.

'Joseph Keneally, you look like a grot. Shift your arse. We've got an hour until the entrée's ready.'

'You didn't tell me we were dining out!'

'We're not. Tonight, I'm the chef and maître d'. Scrub up and let's get going.'

'An S trifecta, and I'll be with you in a tick.'

'Okay, but hurry.'

Joe rushed inside and left the two girls alone.

'Such a charming man your brother. Fancy having a shit, shave, and shower just for me.'

Dot looked at Margot – the refined Margot. Her friend and ally. 'What do you think his chances are of ever going back to uni?'

'Bank on it, Dot. He's a smart munchkin that brother of yours.

Frankly, his chances for a return to uni, a three-course meal, and me tonight are pretty good.'

Dot stifled a laugh. 'Just make sure you bring him home for breakfast. He still wants to go to the Moratorium tomorrow.'

✳

On the way over to the Surry Hills apartment, Joe quizzed Margot on her newly acquired cooking skills. Before, when they lived together, the only things they ever ate were chicken and potatoes, or cutlets and peas. And everything was always overcooked.

'Well, there's something I haven't told you. I'm living with a man who is a bit of a chef. I learnt it all from him.'

Now she had Joe's attention. 'What? You're living with another man!'

'Well, you insisted on staying at Day Street while you recovered. What's a girl gonna do?'

Joe didn't know what to say. Margot laughed so much, she almost lost control of the car. 'It's not quite what you think. So, here's the heads-up before we get there.'

'First thing: he's as camp as a row of tents. Second thing: he's renting one of the spare bedrooms while his semi up the road is being renovated. Third thing: His name is Randolph Saxe-Coburg. He's quite a dandy, and he claims to be related to English royalty. He certainly dresses and acts like he is. And the fourth thing is: He's Randy by name, and Randy by nature. The procession of men frequenting his bedroom is overwhelming. I can only imagine what it's for. Fifth thing: He's moving back to his own place next week for good. I'll be lonely Joe. You wanna come keep me company again on a more permanent basis?'

CH 37 – FRANK – THE MORATORIUM

1970

Frank had seen the blank, unfocused gaze of many of the returning Vets – WW2, Korea, Malaya, Borneo, Vietnam. He observed Joe across the breakfast table. The thousand-yard stare was not part of Joe's arsenal. His eyes were keen, sharp, edgy – and it had always been so since he was a young boy. What was different since he got back from Vietnam was the addition of a certain sensitivity and empathy, not only in his eyes, but in his actions. Frank wondered if it was war that had made it happen. Whatever it was, he liked what he saw. Today's Moratorium would put it all to the test.

'What's the feeling like over there, about the strikes and the anti-war protests back here? Surely our guys are getting edgy.' Frank hadn't planned to say it exactly like that, but it was done now so he waited for Joe's response. When it came it was measured like his letters.

'It doesn't seem to affect the soldiers while they're over there that much. We have each other, and our time in Nam is shared by everyone there. There's even talk among some of the nashos that if they were to be called home, they'd re-enlist as regulars to stick with their mates. But getting back here in Oz it's a different story. I can't say I wasn't gutted by the protests I saw at the airport. And all the placards and graffiti in town. It's one thing to voice anti-war sentiment, but to directly blame the troops for murdering and raping innocent villagers is reckless, ill-informed, and just plain stupid. That's why I want to go to the Moratorium to get a first-hand idea of what's going on back here. Maybe it's the psychologist in me. The soldier too.'

There was another uneasy pause. Frank spoke first, 'Can I come with you, Joe? I've got some time up my sleeve if you'll have me?' And as if to reinforce the role of the father asking permission from the son, Joe leaned over and pretended to snatch his father's ear off, showing it to him in his cupped hand. His dad remembered he used to do the same thing with Joe's nose. Funny, Frank thought, for Joe go for the ear instead.

'Sure dad. Come along. It'll be good material for my dissertation, if I ever get to doing what Hops wants me to do. Maybe you can give me an angle. Margot has loaned Venus to me for the day. I'd rather take the bug than your Cortina anyway. And besides, the lady beetle's PEACE messages should allow me to park safely inside the grounds of the university. The rally starts on the front lawn opposite the quad. We march from there.'

Dot and Winn made their way into the kitchen. Late by design, Frank thought.

'Have a nice dinner with Margot?' his sister asked with a snigger.

'Yes, thanks Dot. Pass the sugar.'

'It's a bleak old Friday for the rally,' mused Winn. 'Both of you, be sure to rug up.'

The boys didn't mind being *mothered* occasionally. They didn't have long together before Joe would be returning to Vietnam and to war. This was a way of reaffirming their bond – as soldiers, as mates, as father and son. Frank's smile said it all.

✱

Joe took the wheel. His father still refused to drive a pink car. Out the back of the house they went, into Therry Street, down Tranmere, left into Day, then right at the traffic lights onto Victoria Road. Winn was right about the cold. And the car's heating didn't work. Never did. Joe could see patches of blue appearing, perhaps a good omen for the rest of the day.

Onto the Iron Cove Bridge.

A red and yellow Datsun coming from the Rozelle side veered over the double lines and headed straight for Venus. Joe tried to avoid it, but there was nowhere to go to escape the impact. His head pounded against the roof of the car, and everything went black.

When he regained consciousness, he was confronted with two bloodied Asian faces jutting through the windscreen of his car. For a split second, images of dead VC and NVA flashed through his senses. He attempted to push away from them, but his feet were trapped between the pedals and the mangled dashboard. He looked past the distorted faces. His father's head was skewed away from him at an impossible angle.

*

News broadcasts on Saturday morning told the story of the Moratorium.

Thousands of anti-war protesters marched to the centre of the city from assembly points at the University of Sydney and the University of New South Wales. Hundreds were arrested. Police brutality was rife at Wynyard Park and Victoria Park. Horses, batons, tear gas were employed. Many of the marchers were injured, some seriously.

Moving to another story, the notorious stretch across the Iron Cove Bridge claimed another three lives yesterday after a head-on collision involving two cars. The lone survivor of the crash, a returned National Serviceman, is in a stable condition in Balmain Hospital with non-life-threatening injuries.

CH 38 – VENUS – A DIFFERENT DIRECTION?

1970

Joe's left foot had been crushed in the accident. Two of his toes needed to be amputated – the little 'pinkie' and the 'ring' toe next to it. The prognosis for the remainder of his foot was good, or so the doctors told him. They assured him his injuries would heal, and his gait would improve over time. But the anguish and guilt caused by his part in his father's death was another story. He kept asking himself, why did he want to go to the Moratorium in the first place? Why did he let his father go with him? Could he have reacted differently? Perhaps he could have steered Venus in a different direction? And on top of all that, he wondered if Winn and Dot secretly blamed him for the accident. He could understand if they did. After all, by cheating his own death yet again, he believed he had sealed the fate of his own father.

Joe realised he wouldn't be returning to Vietnam. He would be doing his fighting on home soil from now on. Ironically, his toes were not lost in the theatre of war. Not by any make-shift toe-popping booby trap. They'd been taken away in the playground of peace. In his notebook he would write: *Peace is a kind of war too.*

*

Joe was discharged from hospital two days before the burial. A distraught Dot pushed his wheelchair to the side of the grave. The headstone at St Patrick's now read:

Alice Enez Keneally 1926-1950. Loving wife of Francis (dec.). Devoted Mother of Joseph. Gone too soon. Until we meet again.

Francis Michael Keneally 1917-1970. Loving husband of Alice (dec.). Devoted Father of Joseph and Dorothy. Adored son of Winifred. A life lived for others. At one with Christ.

CH 39 – DOT & TOM – MOULD & FORMALDEHYDE

University for Dot was in stark contrast to the institutional and religious constraints of the Sacred Heart Catholic College for Ladies. In view of the distress and heartache following the family tragedies leading up to the HSC exams, she was relieved to have made it to university at all. Dentistry was a bonus. She would be with Tom. Transferring to Medicine was still a possibility at the end of year one, provided her grades were good enough. She would see if she'd make the move when the time came. She was grateful that Tom's support made it possible for her to get this far. She would miss him if she ever changed to another faculty.

Dot loved the early morning lectures at Carslaw. They came courtesy of multiple TV monitors with presentations that closely followed the contents of the first-year biology coursework books. Part of the fun was looking around at the guise, the pretence, and the antics of the other students. She wanted to be like some of them, others not. To get the best view, Dot always sat up the back of the sloping lecture theatre.

After biology, she strode across Eastern Avenue to the School of Chemistry, redolent in its own distinctive sulphur aroma. The old Med School next door, where Introductory Medical Science was taught, also had its own smell – this time a mixture of mould and formaldehyde. Early afternoon saw Dot back down to Carslaw physics laboratories where, on her first attempt, she worked out Planck's constant to the 2nd decimal place. She couldn't believe physics pracs could be so much fun.

Music ensembles, sports clubs, political parties, drama groups, the student press – it was all overwhelming. A different racial mix entirely. So too an assortment of denominations, languages, sexual orientations. She realised this time in her life had the potential to make just as much of an impression on her future way of thinking as her formal studies. In addition, she occasionally got to meet up with Joe, who was doing his honours year in psych. And it was good to be there with Tom too, although his attention these days was acutely focused on two particular girls he knocked around with – a blonde from Pharmacy and a brunette from Medicine. Good for him she thought, as long as he doesn't forget about me.

1972

Anatomy in 2nd year was unforgettable. Dot was nervous before her first day of cadaver dissections. The sight of white sheets covering several corpses laid out on cold, hard slabs was daunting enough. Then there was the scent of the embalming fluid hovered in the air. She was issued with latex gloves and assigned a station. Four others were with her at the dissection table. First, there was a moment's silence to honour the people who had donated their bodies. The sheets were folded back. Two students fainted immediately. Another couple succumbed in the first few minutes. One of the male students on Dot's table was greeted face-to-ghostly-face with his former piano teacher, cold and solemn. He was assigned to another station. Tom, ever observant, offered to be his replacement, a strategic manoeuvre producing a familiar knowing smile and wink from Dot.

Tom also volunteered to make the first cut. Typical Tom, thought Dot. Everyone became focused on the task at hand despite the smell of the formaldehyde and the unfamiliarity of cutting into human flesh. After the first hour or so Dot was amazed at how she and the others at her table had become comfortable with the situation, so much so that it was not long before students from different stations started circulating around the room to get a sense of the plethora of anatomical variations amongst the bodies.

On Dot's own table, Tom was having a difficult time peeling back the skin of the scalp. The anatomy tutor encouraged him by suggesting he was being too delicate. 'Be more deliberate,' was his advice. Emboldened, Tom delved into the subcutaneous tissue, filleting along the bone of the skull, realising he was opening a new chapter of his life. He was rewarded by the instructor's ironic aside, 'Congratulations gentlemen and lady, your group has scalped its first cadaver.' By the end of the session, it was time to clean up, fold back the disturbed muscles and skin, brush on more of the embalming fluid, and talk about what had been found and not found over a cup of coffee or a pint of beer.

For Dot, the other practical disciplines did not rate with the fascination of operating on the human body. Histology and physiology pracs didn't have the same pizzazz for her, although Tom's enthusiasm for physiology – what he described as his *'ministrations and outright augmentations'* – were, according to his own critique, *'astounding feats of adroitness to behold'*.

After the preliminary few weeks on campus, it was time for Dot's first trip down Parramatta Road to the Dental Hospital, the unusual-looking pink triangular building in Chalmers Lane, Surry Hills. For all the newbie dental students it was a realisation that it would be at this very building they would become practicing clinicians, working on their own patients, providing health care in a very tangible way. And it would start with immersion into the prosthetics laboratory – investing gypsum, carving wax, casting metal, bending wires, polishing greenstone casts. Of course, in the process of carrying out these actions, injuries and embarrassment were suffered with honour – the burning of skin on red-hot wax knives, the splitting of the webbing between fingers, the catching of hippie-hair on spinning drills. The pleasure and the pain of the prosthetics lab would be an apt introduction to the experience of being a dentist. Dot couldn't imagine being anywhere else. With anyone else.

CH 41 – JOE – A CUP OF TEA

1972

I'd just got back to Surry Hills. Margot had set the table. Champagne was waiting in the fridge. It was Friday 21st July, my birthday. Twenty-four years of age. Honours year done and dusted. Master's in clinical psychology underway. Margot had been promoted to a senior researcher's position at the New South Wales Institute of Health. Finally, things had started to settle.

The phone rang. It was Dot. 'She's dead Joe. Nan Winn is dead. What do I do?'

'I'm coming over straight away, Dot. Take a seat on the veranda and wait for me. Don't go back inside.'

The Cortina was in the street close by. We got to Day Street in twenty minutes or so. Parked out the front. Ran up the steps to the waiting arms of Dot. She clung to me. Sobbing. Wouldn't let go. Margot embraced the both of us. Dot stayed with Margot while I ventured inside. I saw Winn's feet at the entrance of the kitchen. One of her slippers had been dislodged. She had collapsed onto her back. Eyes still wide open. She was cold as ice. It must have been sudden. She still had the tea towel in her hand. A broken dish on the floor.

I rang the relevant authorities, but not the parish priest. Winn had shelved religion since the death of her son. She'd told me only last week that God had turned his back of her. And she had done the same to him. She said it was all *hocus pocus* anyway, and she wouldn't tolerate it anymore. Poor Winn. Her son's – my father's – death had affected her badly. She had become argumentative, vague, and doddery. I left her as she was. Made a cup of tea for Dot and Margot. Took it out to the veranda, just as the police and doctor arrived. Dot stayed with Margot and me for the next few days while arrangements were made for the funeral and burial. In the absence of any significant medical history, an autopsy was required to establish the cause of death.

*

Post-mortem findings indicated Winn had suffered a massive heart attack. The left anterior descending coronary artery had been totally blocked. The death certificate had referred to it as the *LAD widow maker*, but women obviously get it too. Winn's passing had come swiftly. If there had been any warning signs leading up to it, she hadn't mentioned them to anyone.

Despite Winn's wishes to the contrary, I arranged a small ceremony at St Patrick's. To me, it seemed the right thing to do. I was told the burial would be one of the last at the cemetery because it was about to be closed and heritage listed. In addition, the multiple burials on the Keneally side of the family plot meant that the only place Winn could be buried was on the Hewitt side. Iris and Winn would have quite a natter in the afterlife, just far enough away from my mother to prevent her eavesdropping.

I didn't know what to put on the headstone. Nan Winn had been a rock for all of us. No words could even start to tell the story. We had shared so much. But there were things I had not shared – stories of the war, and other things. What things had she not told me?

In the midst of life, we are in death.

Iris Victoria Hewitt 1903-1947. Wife of Donald (dec.). Mother of Alice (dec.). Rest in Peace.

Winifred Celie Keneally 1894-1972. Wife of Connor (dec.). Mother of Francis (dec.). Grandmother of Joseph & Dorothy. Always loving. Always loved.

CH 42 – DOT & TOM – THE SECRET LABORATORY

1973

Dot and Tom were now in the 3rd year of a five-year dental degree. Dot was back at Day Street. Tom was there too. He had taken the opportunity to move out of his parents' house for two main reasons.

One was to break away from the escalating bizarre comments they were voicing on race, politics, religion, music, climate, sport. Just about anything, but especially race and colour. They even criticised the way he cut the grass. According to his father, 'The lawn and garden are too damn manicured. The neighbours must think we live in some kind of poofta's palace.'

The other reason was Dot. She was his best friend. Tom wanted to be her in-house mate, but definitely not her in-room mate. That would spoil things. He reasoned he'd be good company for her, and she good company for him. He told her he could help her with any work that needed to be done around the house – gardening, painting – like he once did for his folks. 'We can help each other with our studies too.' They had shared so many things over the years – playlunch at kindy, First Communion, band practice, study for the HSC. Now dentistry. Time and circumstance had brought them closer together than any intimate goings-on could have ever done.

Dot had her own bedroom. Tom had his. But they also shared a study space in the middle bedroom, and a dental laboratory in the basement. The lab itself was fitted out with propane gas burners, electric motors, prosthetics handpieces, and a variety of other useful accessories. This would be their secret setup, out of bounds to any academic competition from their peers.

Frank and Winn had bequeathed their assets to Joe and Dot, which meant brother and sister were now joint owners of the Day Street property. The remainder of the inheritance, which included stocks, was largely saved for special purposes such as, in Dot's case, the purchase of a second-hand Holden Torana. It was in this *green machine* that Tom and Dot made their way to early morning lectures at the United Dental Hospital. At other times, they took the bus and walked through the long tunnel under Central Railway Station, up the steps to Chalmers Lane, past the Journo's Club, and then on to the UDH for pros, operative, and preventive. Then back again to Bosch and Royal Prince Alfred Hospital for pathology and bacteriology. Their time 'on campus' would come to an end soon enough. One day Tom suspected they would recall with wistful affection the codified jars of embalmed organs, the hours studying sections of diseased tissues through the lens of a microscope, the BCG inoculations, the immunology lectures given by Professor Keates – Tom called him '*Spiro*' after the bug that caused syphilis – and the misty Friday evening parties at the Refectory, the ones with María Juana as special guest. The UDH would be their university home for the next two years. And if even a fraction of what the final year students told them proved to be true – about the eccentricity of the building, the staff, the patients, and their fellow students – they realised they were about to embark on an amazing journey.

CH 43 – DOT & TOM – END OF EXAMS

1975

Tom handed in his *Dental Jurisprudence* booklet and looked around to see how many of his year were still writing. Only a few. Dot would be waiting outside. She always seemed to finish before him. He felt light-headed as he exited the room. It had finally hit home. The end of five years. The final exams done and dusted. It was time to celebrate!

The memo for the festivities had been posted on the noticeboard adjacent the MacLaurin Hall foyer. Dot was already well versed with what was in store. Tom checked it out, then joined her. The obligatory pub crawl would start at the White Horse Inn around lunchtime, then carry on to Watsons Bay in the late afternoon. For those still standing, the Coogee Bay Oceanic would nurse them on until midnight. After that, it was Kings Cross for the stayers. Tom and Dot only made it to the end of the Watsons Bay stint. That was enough for them. Tom found out the rest of the news next morning from one of his oral surgery mates.

Amazingly, no one was arrested. Two students were cautioned by police for brown-eyeing a busload of senior citizens on their way back from playing bingo at the RSL. Tom wasn't surprised when he heard who they were. A third student had been lucky to avoid getting hit by passing cars while rapping in the middle of Oxford Street. No surprise there either. Overall, it was an unbelievable result given most of the boorish behaviour had passed under the radar of the constabulary.

✷

One month later the results of five years of study – six or more for some – were pinned up on notice boards in the quad adjacent the Great Hall. Tom scanned the listings through the space between two sweat-soaked shoulders. He came to the 'Ks' first. Dot had passed with honours. He turned around to tell her, but she'd become lost in the odorous jam of would-be dentists. Dot's smaller frame had already circumvented him to the front and scrutinised the results. She found Tom four rows back still looking for her. She hugged him until he was gasping for air.

'You don't know what you got yet do you? I think you may have topped the year. Three high distinctions and four distinctions out of eight subjects. You're a brainiac, Doctor Tom! I'm over the moon with my own results. Not quite the same as you, but good enough to get the position I wanted at the hospital.'

Marty, one of Tom's friends from his pros group, joked to them as he passed by. 'Did you and Dot bribe the examiners or something?'

'Yes mate. We're still paying the bastards off. Would you be good for a loan?'

Marty raised a chuckle. 'Not funny, Tom. I got a conditional pass in operative, which means I have to do supervised time in January before I can call myself *Doctor*.'

'Graduation isn't until February, Marty. You'll be there with all of us.'

'I hope you're right, Tommo. Anyway, what are you two up to next year?'

'Dot's going to stay on at the UDH in staff operative. I've been accepted into the periodontics postgrad program, subject to my results today. Which means I should be okay.'

'Lucky you. More study. You'll be a specialist gum gardener in no time Tom. Bad breath, lots of blood and pus. Good choice! Actually, and despite your alleged bribes to the markers – which by the way should see you doing serious time in Long Bay – congrats to both of you. Let's party on, nonetheless. Are you off to the pub now?'

'Thanks anyway, Marty. But no. Dot and I have a celebration at our own place tonight. In addition to our dental results, Dot's brother is a fully-fledged clinical psychologist as of yesterday.'

'Have a blast Tommo. I'm off to get wasted. See you in Feb. I hope.'

*

'New qualifications, birthdays, Christmas – December is a big one for all of us Joe, especially this year. By the way, we won't be cooking tonight.' Dot smiled and shifted the phone to her other ear. 'We're having take-away from that new Italian restaurant I told you about on Lyons Road. They've had rave reviews in all the papers. I've already ordered for tonight and paid for it. All you have to do is pick it up on the way over. It'll be ready at seven sharp. I'll give you the address. The wine's already here waiting to be uncorked.'

'I'll be drinking Margot's share of the vino tonight. We have news to tell you.' Dot already knew what the news would be, but she didn't let on. Margot had told her a few days before. Fingers crossed for Margot, she thought. A miscarriage last year. She prayed this time everything would be okay. Their son Richie was now two years old. He would love to have a playmate.

Dot and Tom had set up a long table in the backyard. Multi-coloured lights were suspended from the guttering. Streamers and balloons dangled from the Hills Hoist. The balloons displayed their colourful messages: *Happy Birthday! Congratulations! Salutations! Merry Christmas!*

✳

Tom went to retrieve the present he'd been hiding from Dot. He hoped she would be surprised. The original case was a bit of a giveaway, so he packed it in a large box. He emerged from the back door and placed the box in front of her. 'This is for you, Dr Dot. God knows how I would have ever got through dentistry without you.'

She seemed surprised. But then Tom knew she was a good actor when she needed to be. 'Shouldn't we wait until Margot, Joe, and Richie come?'

'Not this time. This is our moment. Just between us. We can put your present away before Rich comes to meddle with it. You know what he can be like. He's two years old after all!'

Inside the box was another box. Inside the second box was a guitar case. Inside the guitar case was a Martin D-28 acoustic guitar. In a quivering voice Dot managed to say, 'Neil Young and Bob Dylan use one of these.' She became teary and gave Tom a kiss on the cheek, then a big squeeze. 'I want to play it now. It's only 6:45. We have time.'

'I have a tuning fork and capo for you as well. This time, unwrapped.' Tom retrieved them from the flip compartment in the case.

Tom went inside to get his trusty Gibson. He knew how well Dot could sing and play. Back in the days of *Acumen* they'd combined to perform a few folkies of their own. He started the melody. Dot joined in. They knew the words so well. Dylan's song rang out loud ...

For the times they are a-changin'

✶

Margot's Cortina inched down the back driveway from Therry Street and stopped in front of the carport. Joe emerged from the passenger's side nursing dinner. Margot unhooked Richie from his car seat, and he immediately ran over to play with the guitars. Tom quickly exited them to a 'safe-haven' inside, returning with a soccer ball to divert Richie's attention. Thankfully, it worked.

Dot focused on finding the semblance of a baby bump. Margot tried to hide her smile, then pulled her dress tighter to reveal what Dot was seeking. 'Oh Margot. I'm so happy for you both. All four of you.'

'Let's not get too far ahead of ourselves, Dot, but so far so good.'

Joe went into the kitchen to unpack their take-away dinner. Printed on the pizza boxes was the restaurant's name, *The Sicilian*. 'Come into the kitchen and get what you want. We'll all eat outside. The table is set.'

One of the pizzas was a traditional Sicilian-style *sfincione*, square and thick. The other one was a classic margherita. Baked *anelletti timballo* was in the plastic container next to the pizzas. The remaining foil contained garlic bread. 'Dig in guys, while it's hot.'

Richie was happy to nibble on the food Margot had brought with her. 'He loves crumbed chicken and diced apricot. And he still likes his milk and bread. That should fill him up.'

'We have much to celebrate tonight.' Joe stood and raised his glass of red. 'We have two dentists at our table, which is good in case one of us breaks a tooth on the pizza crust. We also have a pregnant lady. I am honoured to call this lady my wife. We have a beautiful son who has refrained from turning on a tantrum tonight, at least so far. Well done, Rich! And I am pleased to announce I have secured rooms for my private psychology practice at Sutton Place, on the corner of

Lyons Road and Victoria Road, not far from here. In addition to all that, I have reconnected tonight with an old friend from times gone by, none other than the manager of the restaurant that cooked our meal tonight. *The Sicilian* is in fact run by a Sicilian. His name is Alberto, but I call him Scotty, the same Scotty I mentioned in my letters from the Dat. He's a mean player of the bagpipes too, provided you don't mind poorly played highland music and the bag squeezed on the wrong side. It still sounds the same. And he no longer wears a kilt and sporran, except on very special occasions.'

By 9:30 it was time for the trio to leave. Dot could see Richie was overdue for his sleep. She thought Margot needed a good eight hours shut eye too. Joe was already wined out and had started to slur his words while getting emotional on all matters family. Dot gave him a big hug, then helped him to the car. She had to laugh as Joe and Richie waved good-bye from the back seat. They reminded her of a couple of junior schoolboys on their way home from a footy match.

*

Dot turned to Tom, raised her glass and smiled. 'That all seemed to go well don't you think? Let's do the clean-up in the morning. But for now, how about we chill?'

'Will I go get the guitars?'

'No Tom, not now. Maybe it's time to think back on the highs and lows of those last couple of years before we turn in. What stands out for you, Dr Tom?

'You first, Dot. Give me time to think.'

'Well, it's obvious that some of our stories are bound to overlap. It's hard to forget when both of us were called in straight after New Year's Eve. It was quite an introduction to our final year. We treated all and sundry evacuated from Darwin after the devastation caused by Cyclone Tracy. Almost everyone I tended to had head and facial injuries – broken teeth, contusions, lacerations. It was horrible, but I was so glad to be able to help. Many of the evacuees were my own First Nation's people too.'

'Yep, I often think about our part in that. It was one of our "highs". But then, not long after that, there was a "low" when our mate Jacko had a meltdown at the back of the pros lab. His denture setup hadn't gone the way he wanted. He poured monomer over his articulator and wax up, and set them both alight. And when I tried to put the fire out, he threatened to kill me with his plaster knife.'

'He was crazy enough to do it too, Tom. We never found out what happened to him did we?'

'Nup. Security restrained him, took him away, and he never came back.'

'Speaking of meltdown and fire, do you remember when I burnt my patient's trousers doing the culture test for that troublesome root canal? Test tube and the cotton bung under the Bunsen burner, but I did it in the wrong order. Far out, I can't believe I did that!'

Dot laughed. 'I'm surprised you were let back in the clinic after that one, Tom. Convicted arsonists like you seldom get a second chance.'

'And do you remember that bossy nurse in charge of the fifth-floor operative clinic? All my allocated patients, unlike yours Tom, were either black or coffee coloured. I asked her to send me a few white ones for a change. And when she finally did, I got this weirdo who refused to have any local anaesthetic. Instead, he wrapped rubber bands around his fingers and wrists. And funnily enough, it worked! I never had to give him an injection as long as he had his rubber bands with him. And then I did that Class 2 gold inlay for him, and dropped it while I was polishing it. And the gold flecking on the floor of the clinic made it impossible to find. Finally, when I thought I'd located it, it turned out to be somebody else's from the previous session. I never found out where it went.'

'Frustrating times, Dot, but good times too. I know you got a distinction for the second one. Practice makes perfect! And Dot, that student conference in Adelaide. The one you decided not to go to. Mind you, you might not have cared for some of the shenanigans we guys got up to. You know the story, about how six of us, in our inebriated state, thought it'd be a good idea to relocate a "no parking" sign – complete with its concrete base – to the dormitory hallway on the first floor. Next morning, no-one could move it, let alone lift it. How we hoisted it up two flights of stairs the night before is still a mystery!'

'Funny. Maybe I should have been there, Tom. But before we get the guitars, how about I hear the one about the prisoner.'

'You know it by heart, Dot. I've told you often enough.'

'Remind me just one more time.'

'Well, as you know, I needed to treat him for an acute abscess on his upper central. He came into the clinic with that corrections officer and was handcuffed to the chair. I completed the emergency treatment and was trying to explain to the guard what I'd done. Then I recognised him as one of the referees from World Championship Wrestling. I told him how much I liked watching it on TV every Saturday. Killer Kowalski and the "claw hold". Mark Lewin with the "sleeper hold". By the time I got to the Italian Stallion and the Golden Greek, the prisoner I'd just been treating had slipped his handcuffs down the arm of the chair and escaped. I wonder if they ever caught him? I've been too embarrassed to ask.'

CH 44 – DOT – BATMAN LIVES

There are four key players in the clinic. It is Dot's first year as a fully qualified dentist.

Player One is Torren Davis, the patient.

He has collapsed. No pulse. His heart has stopped. He had been fine during the whole dental procedure. Routine mandibular block. MOD amalgam on his 46. Dot and he had been talking about Tolstoy's *War and Peace* and Orwell's *1984*. The chair was raised. He slid to the side. Said he felt a bit funny. Stood up, and fell to the floor.

Player Two is Dot, or Dr Keneally as she is known in the Operative Clinic.

She makes sure Torren's airway is patent. He is unresponsive. The emergency alarm has been raised. Dot pumps away at his chest, stirring his sleeping heart. Pushing blood to the rest of his depleted body. She repeatedly compresses his chest and hears a rib crack.

Player Three is the nursing sister in charge of the floor, Sister Matilda Martin.

Tilley forces life-giving oxygen into Torren's lungs. Methodically, she squeezes a transparent bag that leads to a tube down his throat.

Player Four is the Head of Staff Operative Dentistry, Dr Reginald Smith.

Reg has the defibrillator and is about to restart Torren Davis' heart.

*

At the end of the day Torren is sitting up in bed, chatting to the nurse in the coronary care unit of Royal Prince Alfred Hospital. He says to her, 'You can call me Che, or Batman. Lots of people still do. They've been calling me those names for years. It's a long story.'

Tilly is back in her Harris Park apartment feeding her two cats and preparing a meal of sausages, beans, and potatoes for herself.

Reg is playing competitive squash against one of his fiercest club rivals at North Ryde Sports Centre.

Dot is at home with Tom. She tells him about her day at work. He listens intently and reassures her how well she reacted in the emergency. He tells her about his research and asks her if she has enrolled for the Fellowship primaries. He plays her a song by Baby James Taylor – *How Sweet It Is*.

1976

The first time I saw Scotty in Oz was when I picked up the take-away dinner for the family last December. I'm not sure why, but I didn't try to catch up with him afterwards. There were excuses. The premature birth of my baby son, Connor. Establishing my psych practice. Lots of niggly medical issues too. Scotty didn't contact me either. Maybe we just didn't want to reopen the wounds of Nam.

Then I bumped into him outside the greengrocers on a cold July afternoon. I'd finished my day at the practice and was about to make my way back to Surry Hills to have an early dinner with Margot and the boys. I heard his booming voice before I saw him.

'Hey Shrink, don't you think it's time we got together? *The Sicilian* is quiet on Mondays. Come over for a yarn. You know where it is. I live up top. Give me a buzz around six.'

I couldn't refuse an invitation like that from the esteemed Alberto Lombardino. I rang Margot and told her I'd be catching up with my old mate from Vietnam. She understood. She thought it would do me some good. 'Be careful with the turps, my love. That Sicilian stuff can knock you around.'

I told her I would drink in moderation, and I'd be home at a reasonable hour. 'I'll get a taxi back. Don't worry.'

I had an hour to kill before six o'clock, so I walked up to St Mark's and sat in one of the pews for a touch of quiet reflection. I thought of my dad, and how he'd met my mum at this very place. Funny, when I left, I genuflected and dipped my fingers in the holy water and made the sign of the cross. Somehow, I felt my act of reverence was appropriate, even though it was the first time I'd been in a church since my father's funeral.

By the time I got to *The Sicilian*, Scotty – I have trouble calling him Alberto – was waiting on the balcony. He came down and let me in the side security gate. I burst out laughing when I saw he was wearing his kilt, sporran, and pom pom cap.

He hadn't changed that much since I first met him in Nui Dat. 'These days I don't wear this highlander clobber, except on special occasions like today.'

Inside his private kitchen, nibbles had been prepared by Marco the chef. Chickpea fritters, arancini, baked swordfish rolls. 'Nothing special,' Scotty muttered with a sideways nod, 'but very Sicilian.' As he said 'Sicilian' his left hand mimicked the accelerated blossoming of a flower from below his chin. 'And it needs to be washed down with a robust Barbagalli Etna Rosso.' His fingers closed together.

I thanked him for going to all this trouble. 'No trouble for a fellow warrior from the 1st ATF,' he said. 'Dig in. We can talk while we eat.'

Scotty explained that he got through his 69/70 tour relatively unscathed – physically that is – apart from the gash on his leg at the same time I copped some metal to the side of my head. 'But there are things from Nam that linger. You already know about some of them. Kind of. You were there when Superman cut down those two women. I did something like that on my first tour in '67. I still have anxiety attacks some nights, and I wake up dripping wet. That's why I kept yelling to the S-man not to fire.'

'Another incident happened at Vungers. Maybe it's time you knew a bit more. You remember when Superman and I got fleeced by that little kid. We'd been bankrolled big time for that poker game. We chased the slippery little pickpocket and eventually cornered him, but by then our funds had been passed on to other hands. I latched on to his tiny Asian throat and dragged him into the water. Superman finally hauled me off him, but by then the little bugger had gone limp. He just slumped back into the drink and sank. I'm not proud of what I did. But then Wotto raced into the water and hauled him out. He told me straight away it was going to be okay. I saw Wotto a lot after that. He never mentioned the kid again. Neither did I.'

'Anyway, Superman told me not to worry about the money. He assured me we wouldn't miss the game. It turns out he had financial credit in Vungers where it mattered. That's when I found out the connections he had from previous R&C jaunts. Not because of him specifically, but because of Boris, your predecessor in our hoochie. Boris – his real name is Viktor Karlikov – was a first-rate blackjack and poker player. And despite the melee that followed in the bar that night, we won big-time. We didn't tell you or Blue because you two, being the pikers you are, would have expected us to pay for everything for our hooch from then on in. It turns out the extra finances allowed me to be a bit of a businessman after that.'

'And another thing Blue picked up, but didn't say much about, is that Superman and Boris had a much closer man-to-man relationship than you and I knew about or would have even suspected. Bluey found out on one of his R&C sashays from a couple of his bargirl friends. I recall Blue hinted at it when you first met him. But I didn't catch on about Boris copping one in the *arse*. He actually got wounded well above the hip. Anyway, Superman and Boris – Ken and Viktor – are still a couple. They live together in a modest little cottage in Canberra. But that's a story for another day.'

Scotty hadn't stopped to draw breath. Then again, I'm a professional listener, after all. This wasn't a psych session *per se*, but it could have been for both of us. I sipped my red and was grateful those days in Vietnam were over.

'How do you know all this stuff, Scotty? Do you still keep in touch with these guys?'

'No, not really. But I have my sources from various supply chains for the restaurant.' He touched the side of his nose to indicate a certain secrecy. 'M's the word Shrink.' His reference to possible ties with the Mafia was implied, but the truth is, Scotty has always been one to massage the truth at times, and I wasn't going to encourage him on this occasion. So I didn't take the bait, and changed the subject.

'And Blue?'

'You would never guess, Shrink. He went walkabout after he got back. Slid in the back door of a USQ course in Toowoomba and has emerged a qualified journo.'

Bluey was another guy I'd lost track of.

'So tell me, how did you come to have a restaurant in Drummoyne?' I had to know how this transition from regular soldier to restaurateur took place.

'Well. I came back and married this lovely Italian girl I'd been sleeping with before I left Sydney for Nam. I swapped letters with her while I was over there. You might remember I showed you some pictures.' I didn't remember. 'This, as you know, would be my second attempt at marital bliss. Her parents owned a restaurant in Leichhardt called *Lido*. I worked there. Cooked, washed dishes, chatted to the patrons, cleaned the floors. I really liked the pulse of the place.'

'After a year she left me for another Italian guy. That guy didn't have anxiety attacks like I did. Didn't scream in his sleep. Didn't have rashes popping up all over his body. Didn't scratch them until they bled. And he was good at controlling his temper too. And he didn't threaten to beat her up when she disagreed with him. Can you believe she left me for him? I guess you can. We got divorced without contest. Her parents were so happy about the split, they made me an offer I couldn't refuse. They knew people who knew people. I got a shitload of money to leave the country for a year or so, just to be sure I wouldn't try to get back to her. Her father arranged work for me through some of his connections. I had a job as soon as I got off the plane.'

'Where did I go? Sicily of course. My roots. I headed straight to Palermo. I tracked down some of my old-time mates. They hadn't forgotten their *paranza corta* tricks, and still used them occasionally to get some pocket money. Thankfully, they remembered me as their friend. But small-time crime wasn't for me anymore. After a year I skipped off to Taormina and some high-end business. I saved all my *leave-the-country* money and worked for the owners of some of the top restaurants in Sicily. Didn't always work *in* the restaurants if you get my drift. I flew back to Australia two years later. Got some backers for a commercial venture I had in mind. Headhunted a chef. And here I am managing *The Sicilian.* Chewing the fat with my old mate. Let's open another bottle. This time, how about a drop of *Duca Enrico*?'

I remembered what Margot had said about the turps. The fact is, I have been drinking too much lately, and I didn't want to let her down on this occasion. So I thanked Scotty and excused myself. Told him I'd better get back to Margot, Richie, and Connor to help with the bedtime rituals. Then I telephoned for a cab.

While I was waiting for my lift, Scotty remembered to ask me how I was.

'I'm okay, thanks. I'm good. Things are going really well.'

As soon as I said those words, I remembered the Dreamer used to say the same things to me all those years ago. My dad said something like it too, after he'd met my mum.

'Let's do this again,' he yelled as the taxi drove off.

He waved from the back terrace and lifted a set of bagpipes above his head so I could see them. He shouted out, 'Next time!'

CH 46 – JOE – WHAT I DIDN'T SAY

I've been thinking about what I didn't tell Scotty at our recent get-to-gether. Even if he'd allowed me time to speak – which he didn't – I wouldn't have given him much of the detail anyhow. It wasn't the right time.

I got back to Surry Hills that evening around 8:30. Margot was giving Connor a bath. Richie was in his bedroom playing with his Lego. Rich is such a good kid for an energetic three-year-old. He knows when his little brother needs extra attention. And his little brother needs lots of extra attention.

Connor was born four weeks premature. Apart from being underweight, he suffered from breathing problems and jaundice. He was well cared for in the neonatal intensive care unit, and everything seemed fine when he was released and came home. But now he can't keep his food down, gets dehydrated easily, and isn't putting on weight. Margot blames herself for his troubles because she's had problems with her milk supply and has to bottle feed him. But after lots of tests the doctors have finally pinpointed a condition called pyloric stenosis. Cause unknown. Although Hops tells me it happens to a lot of the Vets' kids. Connor's surgery is next week. The surgeon plans to widen the channel leading from his stomach to his small intestine. We've been assured the prognosis is good, and recovery is quick. Fingers crossed.

*

What else didn't I tell Scotty? Maybe he already knows through his so-called *connections*. I wouldn't be surprised if he keeps a watch on all of us. Perhaps I don't need to tell him about my problems. The operation on my middle ear. The car accident. My dad being killed right next to me. My crushed foot and the loss of my toes. The special inserts in my shoes. The chronic pain. My excessive drinking. The painkilling opioids I take when I'm not supposed to. Margot's miscarriage. Health problems with Connor. Nightmares and flashbacks. The dead and the dying in my head. The stigma dished out by my own community. My frenzied outbursts. The physical effects of Agent Orange. Lack of government and public support. The impact all these things have on my family. My need to see Hopgood on a regular basis for therapy.

I wonder what Scotty hasn't told me.

CH 47 – KEN & VIKTOR – THE COTTAGE

1976

The two men relaxed on the alfresco deck, one with a stubbie of beer in his hand, the other sipping champagne from an old-style coupe. Ken recalled he had once been told that the glass his lover preferred to drink from was said to have been modelled after one of Marie Antoinette's breasts. But he was also aware that the well-worn myth – the one about drinking from a replica of the French queen's assets – was not unlike many of the stereotypical tales concocted about gay men.

The couple's house in Ainslie had once belonged to a post-war immigrant from Serbia. He had owned several dogs and cats over the years, and perhaps that's why the next-door neighbours' two golden retrievers and marmalade tabby loved sneaking through a gap in the brush fence that divided the two properties. Ken chuckled when he thought about his adopted friends' names. The neighbours told him their dogs were called Abbott and Costello, but it didn't take long to realise they only answered to 'Ab' and 'Cos'. The tabby's name was Puss Puss. Sometimes she responded when her name was called, sometimes not. Either way Puss Puss remained elegant, detached, and in control. Ab was handsome but not very smart. Cos was the brainy one though not quite as grand looking as Ab. Ab liked drinking Ken's beer. Cos and Puss Puss preferred Viktor's champagne.

The cottage, as far as Ken was concerned, was perfect for the two men's low maintenance needs. Canberra was where they grew up, albeit years and suburbs apart. To be able to return to their old childhood town-come-city and still be able to work successfully was a blessing for both of them.

Ken had carried out the renovations himself, all designed to better suit the twosome's respective needs. The largest of the three bedrooms contained a queen size bed with built-in robes and storage. Most of the hanging space was Viktor's. His collection of suits, shirts, ties, and shoes overshadowed Ken's own tiny division for his work clothes. The two remaining bedrooms acted as separate studies. Ken's had a sofa-bed, a small desk, and two large bookcases. Most of the books on the shelves were 50s and 60s science fiction novels – Moorcock, Ballard, Dick, Bester, and many others. In addition, and wherever he could fit them, futuristic and psychedelic posters and prints adorned the walls. His Superman comic collection from Nam lingered in the back shed, neatly packed in a purgatory of waterproof boxes awaiting final judgement. Ken had gone off the comic 'thing' once he got back.

Viktor's study was much larger and dramatically different. Ticker tape machines, calculators, and a series of telephones were positioned on a large, curved desk with a spiral bound self-standing desk calendar on the side. A cutting-edge fax machine rested alone on a separate table. Not surprisingly, a tangled web of wires and cables extended in spaghetti-like confusion around the sides and back of the working space. The adjustable swivel chair was an ergonomic necessity for Viktor when he became engrossed on a project for several hours on end, which proved to be a frequent occurrence.

The outside area was Ken's domain. He loved his rose garden and his tool shed. The long driveway was used to house his removalist truck. The display on the side covering of the truck made good use of his army nickname, *Superman Removals. Relocations and Commercial Deliveries.* He and a couple of casual part-timers did contract work, mostly around Canberra, but sometimes they were required to relocate private and business furniture to and from Sydney. When he was away, the house was sometimes empty for days on end because Viktor was often called to the Harbour city to deal with his clients' investments.

When Ken and Viktor were away at the same time their furry friends continued to sun themselves on the deck just in case their day-time parents returned unannounced. But as the shadows lengthened, Ken knew they would return to their night-time address for an evening meal and an indoor sleep.

*

Ken couldn't believe how lucky he'd been to have found his soulmate in one of the most unlikely places on Earth – in a warzone no less. At Nui Dat, Viktor Karlikov was known as 'Boris', after the well-known horror movie star with a similar-sounding surname. And fortuitously he had turned out to be a lot more than a naïve nasho when it came to tallying the odds for poker and blackjack at the Vung Tau gambling haunts. The team of Superman and Boris became well known at the Dat for their frequent financial killings. And so, when Boris was wounded and medivacked back to Oz, it wasn't all that surprising that several of the 1ATF diggers were not unduly disappointed when the renowned R&C gambling partnership was broken.

In civilian life, Viktor's flair as a mathematics prodigy set him up as *the* whiz-kid when it came to data analysis and market projections. Ken had heard from several of his own clients how much Viktor's expertise was sought after by both private and public organisations in Canberra and Sydney. When immediate action was required for on-site handling of market volatility, Viktor was the problem-solving man on the floor.

CH 48 - DOT - HIGH ACHIEVER

Dot knew she was fortunate to have such a wonderful dental assistant. Nurse Kate had a natural, caring way with patients. She would often be there for a friendly chairside chat while Dot was away in the pros lab adjusting a denture flange or attaching a wire clasp.

Kate was an early morning riser. She had to be because she lived at Katoomba and needed to take the 6:09 train from Mount Victoria every working day to get to the Dental Hospital on time to prepare Dot's operatory and day sheet. It was a long journey from the Blue Mountains to Central Station, but Kate didn't mind because she liked reading. She had a thing for the Wilbur Smith series of novels about the Courtneys. She always sat at the same seat in the third carriage and would save a place next to her for her immediate boss, Sister Matilda Martin. Tilley would get on at Harris Park, and the two girls would natter away about whatever was on their mind at the time. On this particular day, they had lots to talk about, both recently back from their well-earned Christmas holidays.

*

Dot's first patient was already in the waiting area, but Kate wasn't there. Reception confirmed she hadn't phoned in sick. Dot wondered if

Tilley might know why Kate was late, but Tilley wasn't at work either. Maybe there had been a snap rail strike. Dot knew it sometimes happened. But before she had time to find out, a nurse came running in from reception with her transistor radio. As the newscast unfolded, a sense of dread worked its way through every inch of Dot's body. One by one, her colleagues gathered around her workspace to listen. Dot couldn't believe what she was hearing. It all seemed surreal.

*

There are reports of a possible derailment at Granville Railway Station. A rail bridge appears to have collapsed, and we believe people have been injured. The police rescue squad is on its way. It looks like one carriage has been crushed, two others have been damaged. There are reports of screams coming from beneath the wreckage …

News just in now from the rescue squads indicates that there have been severe crush injuries and several deaths …

Mobile cranes have been mobilised to assist with the removal of debris …

Rescuers are finding it difficult to maintain some semblance of order in their attempts to remove the dead, dying, and injured from the wreckage. Onlookers have been asked to disburse to allow ambulance crews better access to the area …

Porta-gas leaks have prevented the use of power sawing equipment. The conditions are stifling. It will take a great deal more time to assess the death toll.

*

It was now Friday morning, three days since the train from the Blue Mountains to Sydney had derailed and been crushed by the rail bridge. Dot found it hard to comprehend how as many as eighty innocent lives had been lost in the disaster. What's more, half the deaths had been in carriage three, where Kate and Tilley would have been. Dot kept plodding on with her work, but not in her normal day-to-day fashion. All the staff at the hospital had been waiting for confirmation of their worst fears. Sadly, Matilda Martin and Katrina Turner were included in the afternoon's list of the dead. Dot was only one of many stricken by the news. For her, the shock would remain for a very long time. And the memory of Kate and Tilley would visit her in vivid and unsettling ways. Sometimes like thunder. Sometimes like the whisper of the evening breeze.

*

After Granville, Dot became ever more obsessed with her work, to the exclusion of what many would see as her leisure time. But for Dot, work and play had become one and the same thing. The upside of the hospital environment had made it possible for her to attend many of the undergraduate lectures, which proved to be a timely revision for her Fellowship Primaries. Dot's understanding of the basic sciences seemed much deeper now that she could relate them to clinical practice. She had also enrolled part-time in the Dental Public Health Diploma, with particular interest in the availability of dental services for Aboriginal and Torres Strait Islanders. She would often discuss her views on this matter with Tom. Sometimes he would contribute with his own perspective. At other times he would be remote and unresponsive, deeply focused on completing his own research project before his final written papers and viva voce exams. By the end of the year, Dot's treatise on dental services for the First Nation's People had been finalised, typed, retyped, bound, and submitted. Her objectives for passing the Royal Australasian Fellowship primary exams had also been successfully realised. And she could now do the Finals at the same time as Tom.

*

Dot had just completed her dental treatment for Jacob, one of the many Vietnam veterans that were now being treated at the hospital. By now she knew his family well, having previously seen Jacob's son Adam, who had needed surgical and prosthetic intervention for his cleft palate. It had been an intense two-hour appointment with the ex-soldier, requiring delicate understanding and handling of his dental phobia and general anxiety. She was looking forward to her lunchtime break. But her thoughts of a sandwich and coffee were interrupted by slow-walking, slow-talking Sally from reception.

'There's a man waiting at the desk to see you, Dr Keneally. He says he's a journalist from the Australian Broadcasting Corporation and he wants to talk to you. Sorry, I didn't give you the messages. I was busy and forgot.'

Dot met him in the common area adjacent the reception desk. He was a big man with a warm, beaming smile. He extended his hand to greet her. It was the size of an African elephant's ear. And yet it had the texture of an intellectual – uncalloused, unmarked, gentle. 'My name is Lindsay. I'm sorry to take your valuable time Dr Keneally. I left messages for you yesterday, but it seems they didn't reach you.'

Dot only needed a split second before the penny dropped. He too was First Nations. She thought he looked rather handsome in the well-tailored suit. His reddish hair was nicely groomed. Its flecks of grey gave him a distinguished look. She chuckled, 'You look different out of uniform.'

'Well yes. That's me. Norman Alfred William Lindsay. You may recall our antics at the airport, including the squeeze in the beetle. And I believe I know a fair bit about you already Dr Keneally. Most of it coming from the mouth of a Shrink.'

'Call me Dot, Mr Norman Lindsay. And I will call you Bluey, Blue, Norman or Norm, depending on my mood. I once heard my brother call you a bullshit artist, if I'm not mistaken. He must have been referring to the *you* I don't know about yet!'

Bluey's deep-seated laugh rose from the soles of his Italian shoes. 'I'm researching a piece I hope will be used in a radio segment about certain Indigenous high achievers. And I believe you fit the bill since you seem to be the first female Aboriginal dentist in the country. If you have time, I want to hear about your journey. Perhaps we can arrange an interview at the Journalists' club up the lane. By the way, how is the Shrink getting along?'

CH 49 – KEN – BINH BA

Ken cried out. And despite it being a cool Canberra night, the sheets and doona were soaked through with sweat. His eyes were wide open, but the only things he could see were images of bloodshed. All these years later the battle still played havoc with his senses. Binh Ba.

Viktor was in Sydney on one of his mercy missions to the stock exchange. Fortunate, Ken thought. This latest episode was a bad one. If Viktor was home, he knew he would have been banished to the sofa-bed in his study. He'd wash the bedclothes in the morning. Viktor didn't need to know. He made his way to the bathroom and took another Stilnox.

Next night, the mayhem happened again, only much worse. This time he could see strips of flesh hanging from trees. Limbs and part-torsos scattered randomly over blood-soaked ground. Binh Ba again. Infiltrating his brain. Seizing and destroying him like a cancer.

Boom from the Centurion tank. No hut. Another boom. Walls into rubble. Trap doors. He opened one, sensed a quick movement. Blatt! Blatt! The blasts came from his own assault rifle before he could focus. One woman. Two children. Blown away.

Sleepwalking, he got out of bed holding the wet sheets tightly under his chin. All three victims were in the room. They kept coming for him. He fell to the floor. Three bodies pinning him down. Then more and more kept piling on top of him. Blood seeping through the sheets. He heard Scotty yell something. But all he heard was 'Fire!' He jumped at the sound of a passing car and sat bolt upright on the damp driveway outside. Puss Puss was next to him hoping for some extra warmth.

*

In the morning, Ken walked down to the Ainslie shops. Bought a newspaper. Strolled back and sat in the weak sunlight on the outside deck. He read about the Granville train disaster, eighty-three killed. He remembered Binh Ba, over a hundred killed. He looked down at Ab, Cos, and Puss Puss at his feet. He spoke to them as though they would understand. 'You know my friends, war and peace can be pretty much the same thing.' Cos lifted his head and seemed to accept the notion. Ab raised his eyebrows as if in doggy doubt. Puss Puss seemed quite blasé about the whole affair. She wandered off to sun herself on the roof of the garden shed.

CH 50 – VIKTOR – A CLASS ABOVE

From what Ken had been told, Viktor had never passed a driving test in his life and had no desire to try again. Apparently, he'd had several lessons, forty-one be exact, from a variety of instructors. Many of them had been reduced to tears. Some to panic. One conceded defeat early on in their planned series of lessons and told him if he ever attempted to drive again, he was more likely to kill and be killed than any combat action he may have experienced in Vietnam. Ken agreed with the instructor and vowed never to step into a vehicle with Viktor at the wheel. Viktor respected Ken's sound judgement on this matter, acknowledging the overwhelming risk his poor driving skills would bring to their relationship.

Flying for Viktor was a different matter. It was his special thing. Ken had known this ever since they had met. In Nam he had never flinched at any means of air transport, even in the Hueys. Into and above the clouds, to and from Sydney, were occasions for Viktor to enjoy. The chauffeured ride to the airport and the ensuing flight time gave him the chance to revise his notes and settle himself before hitting the ground running at the stock exchange.

Unfortunately for the couple's shared bank account, the last year saw Viktor's earlier well-considered actions transformed, unsuccessfully, into a series of high-risk strategies. He'd say unsettling things to

Ken. Things like, 'Money's not fun anymore, my love. It's becoming more and more serious. And that's what I intend to make, more and more serious money.' Caution had been cast aside in search of rapid returns and an early retirement. It didn't take long for word to get around about the dangers of his unsubstantiated schemes. Not only did he lose his clients, his own personal financial losses – and consequently Ken's as well – dwindled. Ken never let on he knew about the losses. He accepted them in the interests of keeping the peace. Viktor rationalised that what he was doing would only be a temporary measure, but the situation kept getting worse. What had once been his business strength – his market insights and his mathematical evaluation – had become corrupted by greed and self-indulgence. No longer could he compete with the resources of the big firms like Coopers and Lybrand, Ernst and Whinney, and Price Waterhouse.

*

Viktor remembered his gaming days in Nam. Together, Boris and Superman had become moderately well off in the gambling dens of Vung Tau. Recent losses on the stock exchange prompted Viktor to make amends in another way – one he'd had success with in the past. He was sure his gambling skills would work just as well in Oz as they had at Vungers, if only he could be given an opportunity to get in with the right crowd. That opportunity came sooner than he had anticipated.

The idea of re-entering the world of blackjack and poker had been expediated by a man he'd met at the Tattersalls Club. The impeccably groomed gentleman had been attracted to Viktor's eastern European, chiselled appearance, his tall stature, his dress sense, and his talk of financial success – especially his talk of financial success. Spurred on by the proposition of making *serious* money, his new acquaintance had offered to introduce him to a gambling club on his next trip to Sydney.

The Sussex Club in Goulburn Street was situated above a legitimate bridge club. Viktor and his companion entered through an innocuous door at ground level and climbed twenty or so steps to the next level. They were met by a burly bouncer who usually required some form of introductory code or sign. In Viktor's case, he was accompanied by a club regular.

Once inside the establishment Viktor was astonished to catch sight of a bar, two roulette wheels, six blackjack tables, a series of poker tables, and a craps table. The place was a class above the dens of Vungers. The ceilings were adorned with crimson panelling and chandeliers. And the liquor was free. Viktor couldn't believe how stylish the place was.

*

Over the course of several trips to Sydney, Viktor won and lost a fortune, in that order. He had worked his way up the food chain to the point where the clients were richer, and the stakes higher. The Boris/Superman escapades of Vung Tau were now distant memories. His Sussex Club gambling companion was not only his benefactor, he had become his lover. Randolph Saxe-Coburg – sometimes known as 'Essie' – had made sure his own finances had not suffered in the course of his amorous and profitable time with Viktor. Quite the contrary. After all, Essie had been a long-term associate of Mr Chen Lee, the club's owner, not only as a procurer of clients, but also as a sometime bagman and liaison officer to high-ranking policemen and politicians.

CH 51 – DINO – THE NDRANGHETA

1979

'Thank you, Mr Lee. It's been a pleasure doing business with you. Now that we are agreed on our respective business undertakings, Dino will see you out.'

'I'm grateful for your understanding Mr Roccella, and I appreciate your courtesy.'

Chen Lee made sure Benjamin, his chief bodyguard, stayed close by his side during the discussions. But in reality, a battalion of Benjamins would have offered scant protection to Lee if Roccella had wanted the meeting to take a different course.

Once outside the office, Lee unzipped the sports bag he'd been given, and rested his hands on the neatly packed bundles of notes. He knew his negotiations with Roccella would not be easy, but this time, at least on the surface, it was a win-win business deal. Lee would continue his control of gambling in Chinatown. Roccella would manage gambling over a wider precinct, as well as the exclusive importation of heroin and cocaine. Agreed-upon operations would remain mutually beneficial provided neither party became greedy and tried to undermine the other's interests.

Despite the evening's amicable conclusion, Lee never intended to fully honour the arrangement with Roccella and his associates. What they referred to as 'The Honoured Society' or the 'Ndrangheta', he knew simply as the Mafia. And he was adamant such people could never be trusted.

Lee brushed the cuff of his immaculately tailored suit and thought it was ironic that it should have been made in Italy, the birthplace of the very people with whom he was now dealing. He thought that one day the tables would turn, and everyone would be wearing coiffured clothing made in China. When that day came, he hoped everyone would also be buying their personal contraband from him.

Benjamin opened the side exit of the inner-city premises and cautiously surveyed the surrounds. A limousine was waiting outside the old stadium to take Lee, as it usually did, safely away to his fortress in the CBD. But Lee had one more business initiative to complete on this particular evening, one he did not want his entourage to know about. At least not yet.

'Drop me off here, thank you Benjamin. I'll be fine. That's my car parked across the road. All is arranged.'

'Are you sure you are okay, boss? I'll get out and see you to your car.'

'If you insist, Benjamin. But then you and your men may leave. I have important things to complete to make sure that the arrangements we finalised tonight work. This is one of those things.'

The Mercedes was waiting near the entrance of a dimly lit storage facility in Chippendale. Benjamin checked the car – under the hood and chassis, in the cabin and boot. He opened the door, dusted the driver's seat. 'All good, boss.'

'Thank you, Benjamin. Oh, and on your way home, and since you will be in the vicinity, I want you to pay a visit to our mutual friend Essie. You know where he is. He will assist us with the delivery of our token of appreciation to the official we spoke about.' Benjamin took hold of the tightly sealed envelope, fully aware of its contents and the importance of his task. There were issues that had to be dealt with in parliamentary circles in the coming weeks. Chen Lee was openly attentive to the significance of those matters. The Sussex Club could not afford to be targeted by ill-timed police raids, just when he was expanding the operation. A portion of the cash obtained from this evening's proceedings would assist the passage of a heavily amended bill making its way through the senate.

'Yes boss. I understand. Goodnight. I'll see you tomorrow.'

Lee waited in the car until he saw the three short bursts of light, confirming the warehouse site was safe to approach. He'd been given the location and entrance code for vault number four by his own man inside the Ndrangheta. Just as Dino had informed him, the storage unit was stashed full of heroin and cocaine. He randomly tested the quality. It was all high grade. *Trust no-one* was Chen Lee's catch phrase. He wondered why Roccella hadn't done the same. This was his chance to divert some of the action away from his competition.

Lee secured the entrance to the storeroom and made his way back to the Mercedes. He smiled to himself and shook his head in disbelief. A few more of these deals, and he would be on his way to controlling key members of the police force, perhaps even a few pollies as well who had become disenchanted with their current benefactor. He was about to get into the car when he sensed something, or someone, was nearby. A gloved hand grabbed him from behind. His attempt to scream was quickly silenced. Chen Lee's termination came as intended, with the precision of a stiletto, and the force of a guillotine.

✦

Don Giuseppe Roccella listened with interest to the news report the following morning.

CH 52 – DOT, NORM, & DINO – ONLY A MATTER OF TIME

1980

Bluey calls Dot 'Dot'. Dot calls Bluey 'Norm'. They frequent the nearby Journalist's Club these days. More than social, their relationship has a professional twist to it. Dot is a regular contributor to the Norman Lindsay Health Show on Radio National. Norm, on the other hand, is now Dot's dental patient.

Norm has enjoyed a rapid rise up the ranks of prominent Australian journalists. He has used his considerable story-telling skills, his defence force background, and his Aboriginal cultural heritage to good advantage. These days, he rubs shoulders with colleagues as diverse as Richard Carleton, Jana Wendt, and Phillip Adams. Indeed, on this occasion at the Journo's Club, he's just had a playful chat with 'Mr Movies' Bill Collins about David Gulpilil's part in the 1971 film *Walkabout*.

Dot looked across the table at the well-suited gent with the newly veneered smile, and flicked the rim of her glass to make sure he was listening. 'Unlike you Norm – no offence intended – being an Indigenous Australian doesn't seem to have helped me much at all. Not in the private sector anyhow. I've applied for a dozen positions in dental practices ranging from the CBD to the burbs. There are always excuses. Body language says it all. I have an honour's dental degree, a fellowship, and a diploma of dental public health. I even have blue eyes.' She widened her eyes so Norm could have a better look. 'But I get overlooked in favour of applicants with paler skin. It's exasperating.'

'And then there's Tom. Everyone wants him to work for them. Don't get me wrong. I don't begrudge him getting anything. He's a good operator, qualified specialist, smart as. But he doesn't want in. He's gone back to general dentistry, teaches in the Operative Department – drilling and filling in other words – and works Saturday mornings for my old childhood dentist in the same building as Joe has his psych practice. The two of them – Tom and Joe, Tommo and the Shrink – even have a Saturday arvo drink and go see the Dirty Reds play rugby at Drummoyne Oval.'

'Dot, you sound like you're just a bit in love with Tom. Are you? Fess up.'

'No Norm. You're wrong.'

'Like a brother then?'

'No. Joe's my brother. It's not the same. Yes, I love Tom like a best friend. From kindy through to now. He started going out with one of the nurses on the fifth floor. Pam's her name. I wasn't jealous at all. Always over at her place. Never spent a full night there though. Always comes home to Day Street in the wee hours. Always gets me a midnight tea and brings it to me in bed. A few weeks ago, he went over to her place to drive her to work. He normally wouldn't do that. Caught one of her house mates in bed with her. Didn't come to work that day. Said he was sick. Cried all day and night. I couldn't console him. I cried too. He's better these days but concentrates on his new research project.'

'Sorry Norm. I was rambling. Tom is a good friend, that's it. *Finito.*'

'So, it's okay if I ask you out on a proper date then? A musical? Nice restaurant? That sort of thing? Not tonight though. I'm off to the airport this evening. Flying to the Alice. Something about a baby being taken by a dingo. Anyway, I'll call you once it's all sorted.'

Dot didn't need to answer. Norm knew it was a *yes* by her smile.

∗

Bluey walked to the back subdivision at *Il Culinario* in Leichhardt. At first, he didn't recognise the man at the table. He wore black. Black shirt. Black vest. Black trousers. Even his hair, which was dark brown back at the Dat, was slick-back, oily black. 'G'day Blue.'

Blue looked across at the ex-soldier who had once worn a kilt when not on patrol. He wondered how different this man in black would be to the tartaned joke-teller he had known in Nam. The expression around his eyes was more intense. His skin, weather-beaten. But his crooked smile was the same.

Scotty slid out from behind the bench and hugged the digger with whom he had once shared a beer and a tent. 'Pardon if I put a crease in that fine suit of yours, Blue. How long has it been? Ten years?'

'Yes, mate. What should I call you these days? Is the kilt permanently gone?'

'Scotty's fine by me, Blue. Mind you, people around here call me Dino, as in Lombar*dino*. I believe you are now known as Mr Norman Lindsay, National Radio broadcaster and investigative journalist.'

'Yep. That's me. But you can call me Bluey or Norm, whatever you like.'

'I hear you just got back from the red centre. Anything to do with the Azaria Chamberlain case?'

'Yep. That's the one. Back from Ayers Rock, what we First Nation's people call Uluru. The ABC thought I'd have inside info on dingos, being a blackfella.' They both burst out laughing. 'You know Scotty,

I think it's going to be a witch hunt. The mum doesn't sob and cry in front of the press in the way she's supposed to. The investigators don't have a body, there's no motive, no eyewitnesses. I've filed all that stuff in my posts, but I'm going contra to most of the public opinion.'

'Anyway Blue, let's order and we can talk about other things. The food here is good. It's family run. It's cosy. It's quiet. And I have a hand in managing it. My other one, *The Sicilian,* is a bit posher. I now have an assistant manager there. Paulo Luca. Good man. He frees me up to do other stuff.'

Blue looked around and became conscious they were the only two people left in the restaurant, apart from the chef. The couple at the front table had gone. The front door was closed. Two men stood at the entrance.

Scotty let Blue tell his story post-Vietnam. 'A stint of droving. Odd jobs. Met a bloke in a pub from Goombungee who was doing a story for his local newspaper. About a Vietnam veteran who blew his brains out because his skin wouldn't stop itching. Got to thinking my storytelling was at least as good as his. I could write and report my own stories. About our veterans. About my People. About all sorts of people. I got accepted in the next intake for the journo's course at the University of Southern Queensland. Through the back door in my case. Qualifications in the army. Work and life experiences. Put my head down. Met some good people. Smart people too. Worked hard. Got lucky. And you must admit Scotty, I'm a good-looking black bastard with a certain air of sophistication.' Both suppressed a chuckle. 'My weekly health slot on Radio National has taken off. Sometimes I have to prerecord a few shows if I'm out on the road. Dot and Joe have been on. Also had Dr Hopgood on about PTSD. But I do other topics too. Your turn now, Mr Dino.'

Scotty didn't eat much while he listened. Up to this time, Bluey hadn't had much either. But he knew once he passed the reins on to Scotty there would be enough free time to tuck into his favourite pasta *al forno*. Blue listened while Scotty repeated the story he told Joe four years before at *The Sicilian*, almost word-for-word. Norm was on board with a lot of this from the info he got from Joe, but he didn't let on. From what he'd heard, Scotty's foray with his second wife was consistent with many of the other stories he'd researched for his show. He knew a fair bit about Boris and Superman too. More than Scotty revealed in his story. About Superman's transport business and Boris's unsuccessful corporate ventures.

Scotty's story ended with a promise they'd keep in touch. Maybe even get the guys from the old hooch back together again at *The Sicilian*. They clicked their liqueur glasses to give ascent to the plan. And as soon as the ringing ceased, Scotty became Dino.

'As you may have suspected, Norm, there's another reason I've asked you here. It's a business opportunity you may be interested in. Something that could work well for both of us. You are about to meet an associate of mine. One of my backers in fact. And it's someone who can substantially help you and your career. But I caution you. This meeting you are about to have never took place.'

Dino then stood up. It was a sign for the next move. The front doors of the restaurant opened. In strode three men. The lead man was modestly dressed, checked shirt, cardigan, slip-on shoes. His hair resembled Dino's in style. The accompanying two henchmen were suited, complete with 1920s mobster felt hats. They looked like they'd just emerged from one of the old gangster movies – highly visible and profoundly mute.

'Mr Lindsay, I would like you to meet Mr Roccella.' With that, Dino vacated his position across the table in favour of his boss.

*

The meeting with Don Giuseppe Roccella was brief and intimidating. It ended abruptly a mere fifteen minutes after it began. Norm nodded his head from time to time, but didn't say more than a few words. Roccella concluded with a penetrating glare that left Norm unsettled. 'Of course, Mr Lindsay, there is no need to reply to anything I have said this evening. Nor should you at this stage. Information on this matter, as well as several other societal concerns, will be updated in due course through Dino. Your media investigations and ultimately your career will evolve favourably as a result. My business and your own professional interests will become mutually interlocked in another type of war, a peacetime war.'

He then stood and bowed his head. Norm instinctively did the same. Accompanied by his two-man cohort, and without further fanfare, Roccella exited the premises.

Dino in a matter of seconds changed back into Scotty. 'We'll be in touch, Blue. But at this stage, let's keep things close to the chest. I'll call you a cab.'

1980

Tom opened the Journal of Dental Research to the academic paper he'd been alerted to. There, laid bare before him, was the core of his own master's degree research. The same experimental design. The same findings and conclusions. The sole author of the paper was not him. It was the name of one his examiners. He was not even cited in the references. He placed the journal carefully on the desk, then kicked a wastepaper basket to the other side of the room.

Tom longed for academic recognition from prominent researchers on the world stage. He was, however, only a junior lecturer. To rock the boat at this point in his career would be tantamount to committing scholastic suicide in front of high-ranking members of the university staff. He vowed to bide his time. To gain credibility and seniority in traditional ways. To excel at a top research facility, preferably in another country.

Tom had been putting together a feasible cause and effect study plan that was yet to be proven. About the way certain systemic conditions could affect oral diseases, and in particular, periodontal diseases. He'd devised an experimental design to approach the problem, but because his recent work had been emphatically plagiarised, he was reluctant to provide details to anyone but a select few. After obtaining advice from those he trusted, he focused on three major research colleges for his PhD application – the University of Gothenburg, King's College

London, and the University of Michigan.

After two months treading water at the UDH, replies to his applications arrived within days of each other. All three colleges had accepted his innovative research project, subject to verification of his academic précis and references. In the case of King's College, an attractive stipend and part-time teaching position was offered on the condition he would be able to take up the posting in three weeks' time. Financial remuneration for his appointment at the other two universities was less certain. He accepted the King's College offer almost immediately, without giving a great deal of thought to certain other important considerations.

There were many things for Tom to do in the time that remained before his departure. He realised most of his friends and work colleagues would think his decision had come out of the blue. And then there was Dot. She would be devastated. He was certain of it. The Head of the Operative Department was encouraging and wished him well. Not only that, he promised that the departmental reshuffle would remain secret until closer to the date of his departure. Tom's parents? He rarely spoke to them these days. The retirement home they lingered in made him depressed. He surmised they probably wouldn't even realise he had gone.

Tom waited a few more days before he told Dot. The enormity of the changes his decision would have for her was weighing heavily upon him. She would be at Day Street alone. Maybe she would take in another house mate. Perhaps Joe, Margot, and the boys would move in with her. It was a big house. There would certainly be enough room. How much would Dot miss him? How much would he miss her? Would she want to come to London with him? All these questions descended upon him after he had accepted the King's College offer and booked his one-way Qantas flight to London.

One week to go. Dinner finished. He blurted it all out, more haphazardly than he had planned. Dot ran out of the room before he'd finished what he wanted to say. The voice he heard – his voice – sounded hollow, far away. Coming without empathy from a body other than his own. He heard her crying in her bedroom. *Situation handled piss poorly*, he thought. He felt ashamed. He wanted to go into her room and make things right. But he knew he wouldn't be able to do that. And so, he stayed in the living room and wept.

Next morning the two of them sat silently over untouched bowls of cereal. The first words came from Dot. 'I'm happy for you Tom, but I'm upset you didn't tell me about it sooner.'

'I was scared no-one would accept my proposal. I was worried someone would poach my ideas again. I was fearful of failure. I was afraid of hurting you.'

'The "I" word keeps cropping up, Tom. We've been part of each other's lives for so long. It's been "us". How could you leave *me* out of it?' Dot's tears trickled onto the table.

'I have no defence, Dot. You are my closest friend. My only true friend. I'm so sorry.'

'Then cancel it all. The trip. The research. Everything. Be here with me!'

'I can't. You know that. I can't. Please forgive me.'

Dot dipped her head and went for a shower. Dressed in her room in silence. Drove the green machine alone to the UDH. Came back to Day Street early. Packed a few things. Threw them in the boot and left. Stayed with Joe and Margot a few days. Avoided Tom at all costs. No phone calls. No communication.

The day before Tom was due to leave, the green Torana was back in the driveway. Dot was in the kitchen, preparing dinner. Table was set. Soup simmering. Roast dinner baking. Red wine breathing.

'I'm sorry, Dot. I didn't want it to be like this.'

'I'm sorry too, Tom. I want it to be good between us. Joe and Margot helped me understand a lot of things. Things unspoken between us. Things by watching them. A few years is not a lifetime. Then you'll be back. I know you're taking the right course for your career. But I'm going to miss you so much.'

'I'll miss you too Dot. You are more than my friend. You are my love. I want you to know that.'

That night she came to his room. 'I love you. Don't leave me Tom. Tom, I love you. I love you. Don't go. I love you. Be part of me. Fuck me! Fuck me! Make love to me.'

They kissed in the morning. The taxi came and went. And he was gone.

*

Dot thought she would be able to cope with being alone in the Day Street house. She became moody and depressed during the first few weeks. She put this down to the emotional events surrounding Tom's departure. Then, when she tried to get back to her normal routine she couldn't. Her thoughts wandered. Initially it was family. She remembered the first day she arrived. Swinging around the Hill's Hoist. Joe, brave and protective. Otto on his rounds. Dreamtime stories with nan Winn. Frank her loving father. His death. Joe and his demons. Finding Winn cold. But then Tom moved in. So much of Tom. Tom and Dot. Setting up their rooms. Studying together. The pros lab in the basement. The exams. Postgrads. Tom and Dot never apart. Never apart. Cruel and agonising words.

She knew change was inevitable, unavoidable. She spoke to Joe and Margot about what she would do. Swapping houses seemed to be the best option. It made sense. Joe was after all half-owner of the house. Dot could live happily in Surry Hills, a stone's throw from the Dental Hospital. And she was sure she could get someone from work to share the three-bedder with her.

She knew it was the right decision. Joe, Margot, and the boys would love the extra space. A backyard, park, nearby school. Joe's practice was within walking distance. And Margot would soon be able to return to NSW Health a few minutes away at Balmain Hospital.

Both moves would be easily sorted. Tom's absence was another matter.

CH 54 – JOE – HOOCHIE REUNION

A year or so ago I could walk to *The Sicilian* without much pain. Today I'm taking the car. My foot was okay for years after the accident. Then it wasn't. The built-up shoe helps, but I need painkillers to function most days. One of Scotty's mates gets meds for me on the cheap. The old ones don't help anymore, so I've been taking some Oxy. At first, they seemed to work. Now they're not as good.

*

I pulled up and parked in Gipps Street at the side of the restaurant, right behind the big truck with *Superman Removals* on the side. Scotty told me Superman occasionally couch-surfed at his place when he got into Sydney late. The side entrance was open, so I looked in. I saw the S-man, stubby in hand. I hadn't caught up with the hairy muscleman since getting back from Nam. Scotty asked Boris, but he wasn't there. Probably still in Canberra working on one of his projects. Bluey said he's coming, but he's not there yet. He'll miss the bagpipe serenade. Maybe that's why he's late.

In I go. We're in the back beer garden, and it's just us. No other patrons. Superman pulls his T-shirt up to expose his tattoo, just so I know it's really him. He didn't need to. Less hair perhaps, but the rest hadn't changed much in those ten years. Big handshake, then a bearhug. It winded me for a few seconds before I caught enough breath to laugh.

'Good to see you, Superman. Your truck outside looks in tip-top shape, all primed for the trip back to Canberra?'

'Yes, Shrink. It's loaded with Viktor's computer gear, all packed for the retailers. Nice and secure. I won't be going back until tomorrow though. Staying on at Scotty's tonight. Early start tomorrow. I hear tell you have your own practice now. Congrats. Maybe you can help me sleep. Long story. Not for now. Come on in. Sit down. Stand up. Have a drink.'

Scotty was in his in-between clothes. No kilt, no sporran. But he still wore his cap with the pom-pom. A faint suggestion of the past. He'd asked Paulo and Marco to arrange a special multi-course entrée and a selection of Sicilian wine for tasting. The mains would come later. We waited another half hour for Bluey to arrive. When he finally trotted in, we spotted two notable features. The first thing was what he was not wearing. He was in civvies, not his usual journo's bag of fruit. The second thing was just as obvious. Bluey's cheek was swollen, his right eye partially closed, and the side of his neck was purple and yellow.

'What happened to you Blue?'

Superman chuckled. 'Obviously someone's been instructing you on what you can and can't report.'

'Shrink's sister is what happened to me mate. Took out my troublesome wisdom tooth a few days ago. Just hope this isn't the starts of what she calls a dry socket. And besides, now I'm her flat mate, I've got health advice close at hand.'

I didn't know about the accommodation arrangements for Bluey and Dot, but I let it go through to the keeper. I didn't want to get off on the wrong foot – no pun intended – for our reunion.

'I hope you can still manage some food, Blue. Marco has prepared a tasting feast.'

'Just try and stop me from eating, Scotty. The face looks worse than it is.'

'No Blue. The face has always been that bad. Mind you, the extra colour is an improvement. No offence.'

'You're always loaded with compliments, Scotty. Why are you always so nice to me?'

I looked at them both and then to the others, and I realised I was the odd man out. I had the feeling that Scotty, Blue, and Superman had been in cahoots for longer than I'd been aware.

*

The dishes followed one after the other. Arancini. Caponata di Carciofi. Cozze gratinate. Sarde a beccafico. And a few more I can't remember. All this to be washed down with some quality Sicilian vino.

I confess, I didn't have a clue what all the dishes were. But I tried to memorise the names as they were introduced by Paulo. Maybe I'll get Margot to have a crack at making a few of them back in our home kitchen.

Anyway, what did we talk about? We started off with rugby. Then Superman's continuing penchant for science fiction. Then it was mainly Vietnam, minus the kills. Nui Dat humour. Vung Tau R&Cs. Vietnamese food and the 'dust of life' children. Bargirls and the backdoor shenanigans. The dust-off men. We wondered what had happened to Wotto. We kept rambling on. Boris and his stocks. Gambling and business deals. Hopgood and PTSD. I had a hand in talking about that, although Bluey seemed to know a fair bit about it too. We touched on Agent Orange. Birth defects. I told them about Margot's miscarriage and Connor's gut problems. Then we got onto drugs, flashbacks, and suicides. Once we got to the DFS trifecta, we stopped talking about Nam and our peacetime struggles.

Then we started on about what we were doing in the here and now. After all, Blue was a top-notch journalist. Scotty was a successful restaurateur. Superman was doing well with his transport business. And I was an established clinical psychologist.

So why didn't it all seem to gel? Why was I so anxious, suspicious, left out? A feeling of uncertainty hovered over our hoochie group. What should have been a culinary feast and a celebration of friendship didn't quite come together.

At one point Superman called Scotty by the name of Dino. Bluey didn't react to the name *faux pas*. The others obviously knew something I didn't. When Boris was mentioned, any reference to the gay relationship with Superman was left out. Superman inferred that Boris had picked up his act but didn't elaborate. When Boris gambled, did he win or lose? Not much was said about his computer hardware venture either. And why did Boris' implied prosperity evoke a smirk from Scotty to Blue?

What's going on? Am I paranoid? Is it the Oxy that's making me feel like this? Why didn't Dot tell me about Bluey moving in with her? Why didn't Blue tell me? Am I going crazy? Am I sick?

CH 55 – TOM – ALONG POPPY CAME

'Stay open. Nice and wide. Another minute and we'll be finished.' Poppy heard the burbled reply from the man below. She smiled to herself. She had been in Australia for only a month, and in that time her working visa and qualifications from the UK had been confirmed. This was her first week working as a hygienist at the United Dental Hospital of Sydney. Of course, being the partner of the newly appointed Professor of Periodontics had been helpful, to say the least.

Poppy looked across to the clock at Central Railway Station. She still had another hour to go before she could meet up with her Tom for lunch. Thomas O'Leary's academic promotion had come as no surprise to the department. His research on the microangiopathy of periodontal diseases had not only gained him a PhD, it had also ignited world interest in the previously less researched relationship between systemic diseases and oral health. In addition, his current research project suggested there was growing evidence of there being a link between periodontal pathogens and pre-term births. His return to the University of Sydney would provide the opportunity to explore this association.

Dr George Potts was in the operatory next to Poppy. She knew he was ogling her when he thought she wasn't looking. He had told her she looked very much like Goldie Hawn, only prettier. She couldn't stand his overly supportive advice, warning her not to incur the wrath of a certain departmental administrator, making sure she knew the protocol for instrument sterilisation, assisting her at the front desk for her daily patient record. Of course, she realised he had ulterior motives. She'd been warned he was a married man in name only, and he believed he had a self-appointed roving commission. She saw Dr Casanova's jaw drop when Professor O'Leary strode over to her workspace and plant a well-directed kiss on her lips.

'Hi George. Still scraping roots? Please meet my partner, Miss Poppy Selwood. One day she will be Mrs Poppy O'Leary. That's what I'm hoping.' Poppy felt a warm sense of satisfaction and privilege surge through her body. 'Come with me Poppy. Your next patient has cancelled. I've just checked. Let's have an early lunch at the Aurora across the road.' They walked arm-in-arm past a disarmed Dr Potts. His next patient had just arrived.

*

Poppy ordered the food at the bar and sashayed back to Tom with the buzzer. In the three years he had been away she'd been part of his life for only the last one. She looked intently at him now. Her gaze presided over him from across the table. The sensation intensified as a beam of sunlight struck him in the face.

'At this very moment, you look like Ashley Wilkes from *Gone with the Wind*. Handsome and gallant.' Tom tried to return her gaze, brushing aside thoughts of a manipulative Scarlett O'Hara. But he couldn't put his feelings completely to rest.

He remembered the story Poppy had told him. About how she first stumbled upon him in the King's College laboratory. His head was supported on the bench by his overcoat. He was snoring. He had just completed surgery on four cages of Sprague Dawley rats. Disease and control groups had been sorted. Each rat's ears had been clipped in a particular pattern to allow for identification. And then the rats were returned to their eye-watering, urine-smelling cages in the dungeon of the School of Medicine.

She had watched him sleep, not wanting to wake him. She told him how he had smelt of rat droppings and chloroform, but he knew it was exhaustion that had provoked his slumber. The story had been repeated to him several times. Her actions were in some ways cute, but smart too. She had covered him with her own coat, making sure her name and contact details were clearly marked on the coat's collar. It had worked.

The buzzer rattled on the table. She had ordered a bruschetta for herself and an omelette with caviar for him. Tom sat there looking at the omelette as though it were alive.

'For a split second I thought it moved of its own accord. It must have been the red and black bits deceiving me.'

'Seriously Tom, it won't eat you. You're the one that's supposed to eat *it*.'

'I know, but I'll have to get used to the caviar through it. I've never had one like this before. There was a time when I would dissect every little irregularity or perceived impurity out of my food before it passed my lips. It might be a tad difficult to do in this case. Does that indicate the presence of an obsessive-compulsive disorder? Maybe that's why I'm such a good surgeon.'

Poppy stared at him, not seeing the connection. When she did speak, she changed the subject completely. This was another aspect of Poppy Tom had trouble with. She was seriously serious.

'Did you ever patent that blood pressure tail cuff you invented? You know, the one for rodents?' Tom shook his head. 'You should have. That device is going to be used by a lot of researchers in times to come.' He was about to raise his shoulders as if to say *who cares?* But then thought better of it when he saw Poppy's expression. The usual one.

'Time to get back to work, Poppy. Dr Potts will be missing you.' Tom was the only one having a chuckle.

✳

Tom and Poppy entered the front sliding doors of the hospital. And there she was, joking with the security guard in the foyer. Dot knew Tom had been back a month or so, but neither Tom nor she had sought to contact the other. She had known about Poppy too, but only in the way Tom had portrayed her. His sporadic letters were like Joe's from Vietnam – diluted, vaguely descriptive, but with no sensitivity. Dot turned instinctively to meet him. Tom froze. She froze. In that instant they shared a moment of intense, muted passion, completely void of Poppy's presence. But then, as if a wave of veracity washed over him, he took Poppy's hand and walked over.

'Poppy, I want you to meet Dot, the forever friend I've told you about.'

'Dr Keneally, it's a pleasure to meet you. Tom's told me so much about you.'

'Yes indeed. Friends in kindy. Friends still. Dot let me copy her lecture notes. In return, I helped her with her denture setups. We were a formidable pair. Not only that, Dot sings like Aretha Franklin and Joni Mitchell all rolled into one. At times, I was fortunate to accompany her on my guitar.'

✳

Tom had much to thank Poppy for. His sanity for one. In the final year of his research project both his parents, Edith and Albert, died within days of each another. First his mother from a stroke. Three days later his father suffered a heart attack in his sleep. Tom replied to the facsimile of condolences from the nursing home, apologising that he was unable to return to Australia for the respective funerals. He also extended his gratitude to them for the proposed memorial service and cremation arrangements. He agreed that the scattering of their ashes around the gardens of the aged care facility was appropriate. In addition, he advised he had sanctioned his lawyer to act as executor for his parents' will, which included making provisions on his behalf regarding probate and the distribution of the proceeds of the estate. Tom expected most, if not all of it, would go to the Catholic Church.

The loss of his parents and the separation from his home added to Tom's loneliness. Work had become his only purpose. Any form of social interaction had been put on hold, unless it involved his research supervisor, Professor Nicolas Sullivan. Sullivan's significant contribution to Tom's thesis was geared towards the coherent presentation of scientific argument. Tom's practical skills could not hold a candle to his supervisor's academic guidance, resulting in rational and logical steps towards his dissertation's discussions and conclusion. This was the reason he had come to King's College. The defence of his PhD had been all the better for it.

Tom often looked out the window of his workspace to the day-to-day happenings on the Strand. He wondered if any of the passing parade would understand the path his life had taken. Would anything he was now doing really matter to them? Did his parents ever understand his sequestration from their existence? Catholic guilt weighed heavily upon him, countered only by his ambition and the progress he had made. He missed Dot more than he could have imagined. He was constantly tired and depressed. Thank goodness Poppy came along when she did. For the final six months at King's, she shared his room. There was no question of another alternative when they set off to Sydney as a couple.

✳

The atmosphere at their Waverton apartment that evening was not pleasant.

'*Just friends* don't look at each other that way. You were lovers, weren't you? I can tell.'

'Poppy, Poppy. Why do you say that based on a brief meeting? Dot and I are good friends. And we still are. But lovers, no.'

'You didn't tell me you lived with her. I found that out. And she's black! You didn't tell me that either.'

'How can you call out her colour like that? That's bordering on a racial slur, Pops. I didn't realise you were racist!'

'Pops! Don't call me that name. And I don't care about her colour as much as I do about the fact that you have been fucking her for years. And maybe you are about to start doing that again. Maybe you already have. Have you been fucking her since you've been back? I can just imagine you two going at it hammer and tongs on the desk of your office.'

'I'm not in the mood to fuel this argument any more Poppy. Perhaps you will see reason once you calm down. You are not being rational at the moment. Leave it be. That's what I'm doing now. Leaving.'

'Oh fine. You are the holy one. And it's me who is at fault. Who helped you out when you were down? Who made sure you finished your PhD when you were about to give it up? Who left her home and country to support you in your career? Me, me, me. That's who. And now I find out the truth about you and that Zulu woman.'

'I'm off. See you tomorrow. Maybe.'

'Where are you going? Where will you …'

Tom was out the door before he heard any more. The neighbours from the adjacent apartment were out on the stairs listening. 'Is everything okay?'

'It's all fine. Poppy's just rehearsing her part in *Who's Afraid of Virginia Woolf?* It's at the Ensemble Theatre next week. You should go. She's great. Sorry for the disturbance. She's one of those method actors you've probably heard about. Anyway, I'm off to get some groceries. Have a good evening.'

With that, Tom was down the stairs and off to book a couple of nights at the nearby Harbourview Hotel.

CH 56 – JOE – ON MY MOTHER'S GRAVE

1983

I saw Ken Campbell as a patient about a month after our hoochie reunion at *The Sicilian*. That was two years ago. These days we arrange a session most times he comes to Sydney. I've been fortunate to be able to appreciate a different side to the digger I used to call Superman. He's more like me than I would have expected all those years ago. But there are still many things to discover. About him. About me.

The first time we met on a professional basis I assured him that whatever he told me, and whatever I told him, was strictly confidential. 'Like a confessional,' I said. Although that didn't mean much to either of us, so I said, 'On my mother's grave.'

Early on he talked about his anxiety attacks, the sleepless nights, the flashbacks. The carnage at Binh Ba. The killing of innocents. He'd been using. Pot, cocaine, Stilnox. I asked him where he got it all. He just said he had his sources. I didn't press the issue. The important thing was, he was in the process of gradually eliminating all of it. And his local medico was on-side with my treatment plan.

Later, we spoke more about PTSD, and how for him it had become chronic. He smoked too much. He was always tired. He had anxiety attacks at unexpected times. I told him I had them as well. And that I'd been seeing Greg Hopgood the psychiatrist about my issues. 'Therapists need therapists too,' I said. I think it helped that I was able to admit my own vulnerability to him.

Then he spoke about his relationship with Viktor. They first got together in Nui Dat. Did the Vungers R&C trips. Did some backdoor rumpy-pumpy. Won lots of money too, before Viktor collected a piece of shrapnel and got shipped back to Oz. I heard about Viktor's wins and losses at the stock exchange. And the high-stakes gaming at Chen Lee's gambling palace. He also told me about Viktor's forays into their joint bank account, something he knew about early on, but didn't confront him with because he thought it could end their relationship. But then, over subsequent months, all the lost finances were restored with interest. Ken wanted to believe the extra money came from his partner's computer hardware business. I can still hear him trying to convince me – and himself – that it was all legit.

'He's been working really hard, Joe. He's made so many trips to Sydney to shore up clients. And his Canberra clientele has expanded as well.'

'You have no idea how good it is to talk about these things confidentially to someone, Joe. Thank you. You and my GP have helped big time. My main issue now is fatigue. These long trips to and from Sydney are taking a physical toll on me. I get tired doing all the driving myself, but I don't want the burden of arranging accommodation for my offsiders when scheduling requires an overnight stay. The current system works fine. I have casuals at both ends that help with the loading and unloading. But driving alone is monotonous, and I must admit to you, Joe, I occasionally take uppers to keep me awake. One of Viktor's contacts supplies me with all I need. I used to do coke and Stilnox too, but I've kicked that habit. Viktor says it's all above board. But I know it's not.'

When he said that, I felt my stomach churn. I remember how I used to get my own supply of Oxycodone before Hops helped me overcome that need.

Then Ken turned to me and looked me straight in the eyes.

'Joe, I've got something I have to do. Meet someone. Something I need to tell you about. But it can wait until next time.'

CH 57 – ESSIE – THE TIP-OFF

1983

Randolph Saxe-Coburg sipped his cup of tea and listened intently to the breaking news.

The body of Mrs Linh Nguyen, mother of two, was recovered this morning from an area inside the Birkenhead Shopping Centre carpark at Drummoyne. She had been stabbed to death and her body loaded into a St Vincent de Paul's clothing bin. Suspicions were aroused when she didn't collect her two daughters from school the previous afternoon. Despite an overnight search, her body was not discovered until her vehicle and a nearby blood trail were noticed by returning workmen at the site this morning. Mrs Nguyen is the wife of well-known and respected surgeon Dr Tran Nguyen at the nearby Balmain Hospital. Family members, friends, and hospital staff have expressed their sorrow and distress that such a lovely lady had been murdered in a particularly brutal and senseless manner. Police have not ruled out mistaken identity in this specific case. Alarmingly, however, the detective chief inspector in charge of the investigation has forewarned that there were elements related to the murder that suggest this may not be the killer's first victim. In the meantime, the public has been warned to be vigilant.

Now turning to more pleasant news. The Sydney Entertainment Centre was opened today …

*

Saxe-Coburg switched the TV off and pondered his next move. The situation was tricky. He needed to know how the murder of Linh Nguyen was connected to his scheduled business deal. Was she sent by a third party? Was she somehow involved? Was the assassin ordered there to protect him and his interests? After all, the tip-off came from a reliable source. The victim could well have been him.

CH 58 – JOE – LEAVE IT TO ME

I didn't see or hear from Ken for over six months. He didn't answer any of my calls or messages. I shared my concerns with his GP, who went to his Ainslie house to check on him. No-one was there on the occasions he tried. Then, out of the blue, Ken contacted me. He said he needed help.

When we finally got together, I could tell he had relapsed big time. He'd been taking uppers and downers, sometimes separately, sometimes together. Cocaine. Meth. Xanax. Seconal. All mixed with Stilnox and alcohol to try to get some sleep. I don't know how he was able to drive any vehicle, let alone a large truck, without killing anyone else or himself.

I asked him how things were with Viktor. That provoked an immediate anxiety attack. I calmed him down as best I could, and suggested he see Dr Hopgood to assist with his drug habit. He wouldn't have anything to do with it. So, for the time-being I thought it best to play it cool and work out what issues needed to be prioritised.

'Things have changed Joe. Scotty is Dino. Dino isn't Scotty anymore. Did you know that? He thinks he's Al Capone reincarnated. He keeps passing snippets of information to Bluey to boost his radio broadcasts and newspaper articles. But it's all what Scot … Dino wants him to say. And Bluey goes along with it. I can't work out if Blue is playing or being played. Maybe a bit of both. But it's got to come at a cost.'

Ken stopped for a while and gathered himself. I thought he'd finished. But he was just refuelling.

'And I'm no longer Superman, Joe. I'm Ken the deserted lover. Viktor has been with someone else. Still is. And that's what my meeting was about the last time I saw you. But this Essie guy didn't turn up. Which was lucky for him. Because I found out I've been a drug runner for both of them for longer than I care to know. I've been a fool, Joe. One day while I was unloading, I dropped a box of what I thought were computer monitors. I freaked out, thinking that I'd smashed a couple of screens. It turns out, the only things that were threatened were the seals on parcels of heroin and cocaine.'

'I did some snooping around about what I'd discovered and was warned off by Bluey not to go any further. Blue or Norm, or whatever he calls himself these days, knows a fair bit about what's going on. But he's probably in the same position as I am. And anyway, he's become the go-to media man when it comes to his articles on the Vets, organised crime, and the drug trade. No wonder he's become "Mr Exclusive" by playing along with it. But they know I'm wise to their operation. That's why I made myself disappear. Viktor doesn't have a clue what's happened to me. But I know they'll track me down sooner or later.'

I had a feeling Ken was right. My rooms had been broken into a couple of times this year. First time was a few months ago. And again last week. Nothing taken, but Juliette my practice manager reckons some of the files had been disturbed. She'd had the barrels on the cabinets changed after the first break-in. But they'd been tampered with again. The Cs and Ks especially. Whoever did it didn't know I kept Ken Campbell's records and a few of the other Vet's files at my home office. But with what I now know, I wouldn't put it past Dino and Co. to target *me* next – my family too, God forbid. Everyone I love and believe in. I couldn't stand by and let that happen. Not ever! And I thought about what that priest said many years ago at Corps training. About moral judgement and belief. And ungodly things.

✶

I told Ken to leave all it with me. I had an idea. I asked him where his truck was.

'I parked it in Tranmere Street Joe. It's empty. Walked here.'

Good move I thought. I knew someone that would store it for him locally. Out of sight, but accessible. I filled Margot in on the plan. I needed her help. After all, she was the one who suggested I keep Ken's records separate from practice storage in the first place. Then I set the S-man up in the spare bedroom for the night. It was time to prolong his disappearance.

My sister Dot had contacts in the Territory that could help him. I had contacts there too. There was a rehab facility just out of Darwin. Hops and some of his colleagues had set it up a few years ago. I knew it wasn't going to be easy for Ken. I was honest with him and told him so. But he'd be alive and getting better. I warned him whatever he did, not to go back to Canberra. Our plan could be arranged discreetly from here.

'Thanks, Joe. I don't know how I can ever make it up to you.'

I said it would cost him the science fiction novels I'd been meaning to return to him.

He didn't argue.

CH 59 – JOE – CHRISTMAS DINNER

Tom had become a popular key-note speaker at many dental and medical conferences around Australia. One of these elite forums was a three-day meeting in Sydney hosted by the Royal Australasian College of Dental Surgeons. Only College Fellows or those enrolled for primary and secondary examinations were eligible to attend. The venue for this particular event was the *All Seasons Hotel* with views over Circular Quay and out to Fort Denison and the Heads.

It was breakfast time on the final day of the conference. Tom's day off from lecturing. He sat on the lavish sofa near the window sipping his coffee, pleased his presentations had gone so well. The feedback he'd received was satisfying and a just reward for his academic curiosity, determination, and persistence. Memories of how the findings of his previous research had been stolen were inconsequential now. Plans for future projects were far more important. Just the same, he relished the thought of seeking out the very person who had once been his examiner and plagiarist, and discussing with him the significance of his upcoming venture. He might also mention the large government grant he and his team had received for the project.

As he sat there, a sleepy figure manoeuvred her way from beneath the bedcovers and strode naked to his side. She parted his robe and slipped her fingers down his chest.

'I wonder what people would say if they knew you were tempting me like this.'

'They would say you are a very lucky man receiving all this loving attention. That's what they would say.' Dot then moved around and sat on his lap. 'I don't want this to end, Tommo.' She had revived the name she once called him in kindergarten. He lifted her and walked over to the bed, dropping his robe in the process.

'I have a feeling we will miss this morning's lectures, my love. We must be discreet for now, but not forever. I'll put this right as soon as I can.'

*

Friendly, dependable, and as bubbly as freshly poured prosecco. Juliette was Joe's practice manager and minder. She greeted his patients as though they were old family friends. She knew the names of their children and where they had been on their holidays. She made his patients feel important. And crucially for Joe, she made his life easier. Joe's last appointment for the morning was with Miss Wallis, a long-time participant in his hypnotherapy and relaxation program. Juliette wondered if Joe realised how much Miss Wallis adored him.

'In a moment I will count from one to three. On the count of three you will open your eyes. You will be completely and totally awake. Feeling fine, relaxed, refreshed. Feeling full of energy. Full of vitality. Very, very happy. Full of confidence. Full of ability.'

'I am going to start counting. One, you can feel normal body sensation extending back into your arms and legs. Two, normal muscle tone creeping through your entire body as you come closer and closer to the surface. Closer and closer now. Almost there. Almost there. Three! Open your eyes! Wide awake! Wide awake!

Miss Wallis opened her eyes. She fluttered her eyelids a number of times and smiled at her therapist.

'How do you feel Miss Wallis?

'Wonderful Joseph. Simply wonderful.'

'You are certainly making fine progress. We can schedule your next appointment for after the Christmas-New Year break. Let me escort you to reception.'

Miss Wallis supported herself on Joe's shoulder as she slipped her shoes back on. She thought his longish sandy hair peppered with grey was very sexy, and his gold-rimmed glasses gave him that touch of learned sophistication. She took his arm as she edged her way slowly to the waiting room.

'Bye Miss Wallis. Have a wonderful time over Christmas and the New Year.'

'I will,' she said.

Joe knew she would go home to a lonely dinner and a still lonelier Christmas.

He made his way back to his office and noticed as he passed the hallway mirror the cheesy smile engraved onto his face. He tried to massage it away using both hands and succeeded in giving himself a pair of ruby-red cheeks. He re-emerged at the desk. Juliette noticed his rosy complexion but declined to comment.

'Early mark for you today, Juliette.' He had given her a sizeable Christmas bonus and a nice bottle of Veuve Clicquot to celebrate the Festive Season. 'I'll lock up. Go home and be with your gorgeous family. Enjoy. I'll see you in the New Year.'

Joe sat down, took his padded shoe off and gave his foot a rub. His phantom toes still caused periodic discomfort, but they didn't bother him as much as they once had. And besides, he was now able to walk long distances without the help of painkillers. Kicking the opioid habit had not been easy, but with help from Hops and a lot of self-discipline, it had been successful.

He looked at the picture of Margot and the two boys on his desk. The memories came flooding back. The Orwellian year of *1984* would soon be gone. But before that, it would be Christmas. As per usual, he had left his shopping until the last moment. What would he get them this year? He pondered.

*

Joe was a contented man these days. Now he was off the Oxycodone, he seemed to be able to manage life's bits and pieces with aplomb. Ken was safely out of town and doing well at rehab. His own practice was busy enough without being burdensome. Dot and Norm seemed to have hit it off. He still liked Norm, but not as unconditionally as he once had. There were moral issues linked to many of his stories. And their sources remained, to Joe's mind, shady. And yet, he was glad for Dot's happiness. He loved her so much. But he didn't want her hurt by emotional ties to two men. He knew she still had a place in her heart for Tom. Poppy, on the other hand, was a different story. He didn't like her at all. In fact, few people did, least of all Dot. He couldn't understand what Tom saw in her. She was controlling, anti-social, and devoid of any sense of humour.

And Margot. Margot his rock. She had sacrificed so much for him and the boys. Richie was eleven, going on twenty-one. Connor was eight, looking more like six. His youngest son still had eating problems, despite medical opinion that the abdominal surgery had been successful. He also wore glasses that made him look nerdy, which in some ways he was. His intellect counterbalanced his physical flaws, but that only made him a potential target for the school bullies. Thankfully Richie was his protector. No-one messed with Richie. Not even the teachers.

Margot had seen Joe through thick and thin without complaint. Not only that, she was well respected in the local community for her charity work. The old saying, *if you want something done, give it to a busy person,* applied doubly to her. How she ever found time to set up the local district's meals-on-wheels project was anyone's guess. Her schedule of three days with NSW Health and two days with meals-on-wheels kept her busier than most, but somehow she still found time for her family. Tonight was a good example. Christmas dinner at the Keneally's would be a big deal this year. Tom and Poppy would be chipping in with nibbles. Norm and Dot with dessert. But Margot made it clear that the traditional roast would be her domain.

⋆

Joe looked down at the now-cleared wooden dining table. It was dark and heavy, and the edges were rounded in certain areas, attesting to its use over the years. He knew the history of each scratch, notch, and stain now modestly veiled by a lace tablecloth. The addition of the tablecloth was seldom thought of in times gone by. This evening's Christmas dinner was one of those very special occasions that demanded a certain fastidiousness. The boys were now in bed, although Joe suspected Richie would be at his door eavesdropping on their conversations. And Connor would probably be reading one of his *Biggles* adventure books by torchlight.

Between the completion of the pavlova and the start of the Drambuie, Norm became excessively vocal about the recent federal election. He hadn't expected the size of the swing away from Bob Hawke's Labor Party. But he did predict Andrew Peacock's Libs would be defeated after all. More than once he reminded everyone that 'a Hawke will beat a Peacock every day of the week.' Although he also conceded that 'this particular bird of prey had lost a few of his feathers in the process.'

Dot chimed in when she realised Norm was starting to slur his words.

'Norm's had a big year, as you know.' She put down her glass and counted on her fingers. 'It all started with Eton John's marriage in Sydney. Then it was the Aboriginal and Torres Strait Heritage Protection Act. Then he got caught up in the bikie shootout at Milperra. That should have been enough, but then there was the acknowledgement of the harmful effects of Agent Orange. And more recently, he exposed the escalating drug trade in New South Wales prisons. The Australian Federal Election was the final straw. No wonder he's got a few more grey hairs.'

'Makes him look more distinguished, don't you think? You men are so lucky. You age so gracefully!' Margot pretended she was jealous.

'How about you, Tom? You must be chuffed at the reception you've had since you got back from the UK. And you've found this lovely lady in the bargain.' Joe wanted to sound supportive, but his lack of enthusiasm when it came to Poppy must have been instantly spotted. She turned to Tom with a look of self-reproach as though she'd been caught trying to hide a fart.

'It's time we should be going home Tom. You have a paper to review tomorrow if I'm not mistaken, and I have a meeting with my ex-pat group.' Tom didn't have a chance to reply. They withdrew as quickly as the US forces from Saigon. Norm and Dot on the other hand had been invited for a sleepover in one of the spare rooms. No drive home. And they were in no hurry to end the night's merriments just yet. And so, the four of them – Joe and Margot, Norman and

Dot – chatted on into the wee hours of the morning.

Eventually, as is often the case, the men and the women separated. Joe and Norm made their way to the front veranda. Margot and Dot stayed on in the backyard.

✳

Margot was first to speak. 'Dot, you and Norm are okay, aren't you?' It was a question, not a statement.

'He's away on assignment a lot of the time, Margot. And he has a certain charisma that attracts female admirers. You get what I'm talking about, don't you? And I know for sure he enjoys the attention. He also has a side to him that I'm not privy to. He justifies it to me in a way that doesn't give me a lot of confidence in his motives. He has these secret meetings with what he calls 'informers' and 'sources' that must occasionally have links to unseemly practices inside and outside the law. You ask if I'm okay with that. My answer is – *no I'm not*. He's become edgy, and even aggressive if pressed. And he carries a concealed weapon with him most of the time.'

✳

'Joe, I need to ask you something.' Norm took another sip of his Drambuie. 'I know you've been seeing our mate Superman for therapy. He had a tough time after the battle of Binh Ba. Never seemed to get it out of his head. And then he panicked and shot those two villagers. I know this is in poor taste, but he had quite a collection of ears by the time he vacated Nam.'

And here it comes, thought Joe. He waited.

'Do you know where Ken is now? Surely you must have an idea.'

And there it was. Norman Lindsay, investigative reporter *extraor-
dinaire*, had become a very dangerous man.

CH 60 – D&M, J&T, V&K – OBSTACLES

Margot and Dot went to Misha's Dance Studio on Saturdays. It was Margot's break from the boys. All three of them. The two girls had a passion for dance and rhythmic movement from the time they were children. Margot was classically trained as a youngster. Dot revelled in creative movement. On this particular Saturday they planned to do three classes, one after the other. The first was a warm-up and stretch at the barre. Then *jazz*. And finally *contemporary*.

Dot rushed off to the bathroom half-way through *jazz*. Margot followed to make sure she was okay. She found Dot kneeling on the floor of one of the cubicles, heaving into the toilet bowl, tears rolling down her face.

'Do you need some help, Dot? Food poisoning? Virus?'

'It's a lot more serious than that, Margot.'

'Oh my darling! Are you sure? Have you told anyone? Does Norm know?' Margot noticed Dot had been wearing loose tops to her classes. Her T-shirt fell forward as she stretched over for another retch. Margot could see the evidence of what she now knew.

'How about we call it a day and wander down to Birchgrove Park. Do you feel up to that? We can grab a bottle of water and sit in the shade.

*

Margot was still in her leotards and tights, a tracksuit top thrown over her shoulders. Dot sat next to her dressed in loose shorts and a light shirt. They sipped on their water bottles and watched the cricket. The calm was welcome.

'Norm thinks I'm on the pill. He's still away covering the aftermath of the Victorian state elections. He has no idea. And there's something else I've been wanting to tell you. And you'll be shocked. Please don't judge me. Hear me out. I'm still in love with Tom. You know Poppy left him. She flew back to the UK not long after Christmas. One way ticket, or so Tom said. She won't be missed by anyone here anymore, even Tom. And here's what I've been wanting to tell you, over and above what you've found out today. I've been seeing Tom for months since he got back. And by seeing, I mean we've been sleeping together.'

The silence was deafening.

'And the father is?'

'Margot, I don't know.' She erupted into loud, uncontrolled sobbing. The bowler paused at the top of his run-up to see if one of the spectators had been hurt. The game resumed once Margot waved him on.

*

A few kilometres away Tom and Joe were watching the first-grade game down at Drummoyne Oval. They stretched out on the grass beside the scoreboard. Connor and Richie played on the hill, sliding makeshift cardboard sleds down the slope to the boundary fence.

'I'd better stop them now or Connor's going to crack his head open.'

'Relax, Joe.' Tom was more confident. Richie has control. Wait and see. They're having fun. Richie looked over at his dad and gave the thumbs up. Connor's laughter was the medicine Joe needed.'

'Have you heard from Poppy?'

'Not a sniff. And I don't expect I will for quite a while. If ever. She was there when I needed someone at King's. But the more I knew her, the more I disliked her. She turned out to be a real piece of work, Joe. And the things she said about Dot and Norm, you never want to hear from anyone. Anyway, enough about me. How are things with you? You seem distracted.'

'Yep, I know. It's Norm. I thought I understood him pretty well in the old days when I still called him Bluey. But now he's become more and more mysterious. Short tempered too. He's not the same guy I knew in Nam. There's a dodgy side to the way he accesses some of his info. How else could he keep getting so many exclusive stories over and above his media competitors? He's become the king of scoops. How? And I'm worried about him and Dot.'

Richie and Connor returned with ice-creams from the kiosk. Richie offered his dad the change. 'Keep it mate. It'll be handy for next week. Your mum and aunty Dot will be doing the dancing thing again I expect. We men can be doing our thing too.'

All four of them watched as the umpire gave the batsman out leg-before-wicket.

'Robbed!' roared Richie. 'I heard the nick from here!'

*

Viktor leant over his curved desk. Four computer monitors were in place. The two on the right-side were linked to security cameras that surveyed the outside of the Ainslie house 24/7. The left-side was made up of an Apple iMac and a conventional PC. Both state-of-the-art. He was more relaxed now that Ken was gone. His former lover and the *Superman Removals* truck hadn't been seen for over a year.

Viktor's relationship with Randolph Saxe-Coburg had started out as a sexual adventure. Now they were partners in a major drug trafficking business. Chen Lee had hatched the idea, but he had wanted it all for himself. Essie and Don Giuseppe Roccella had worked out a plan that would be mutually beneficial. Dino had facilitated the whole process, including removing Lee as a major obstacle.

Ken had been an unwitting accomplice for the trafficking. Viktor felt sorry for him because he was a good salt-of-the-earth bloke. But he didn't have even the slightest capacity for anything related to business. What's more, he had already found out too much about the distribution scheme. With all that knowledge he'd become a target. And as far as Viktor knew, Ken may have already been snuffed out by the Ndrangheta on some remote country road, buried in a shallow grave somewhere out whoop whoop way. Or perhaps he'd even been fitted with a pair of concrete boots for his descent to the bottom of Sydney Harbour. Either way it didn't matter. If ever he showed up again, which was unlikely, Roccella and Dino would handle it in a jiffy.

Viktor surveyed the front porch on the monitor. The golden retrievers Abbott and Costello had returned to their usual day quarters now that Viktor was there to feed them. Puss Puss was somewhere around too but the cameras and motion detectors hadn't picked her up yet. The truck in the driveway belonged to a local contractor, another unwitting trafficker moving goods around Canberra and Sydney.

More recently, Randolph and Viktor were working on importing a major heroin haul from Indonesia. This would be big. Roccella's men had assisted with negotiations. Viktor would work on the distribution. Essie and Dino would carry out their side of the bargain in other ways. Manoeuvres behind the scenes were not Viktor's concern.

The monitors had detected further movement in the backyard. Puss Puss was casually making her way to the terrace. Viktor thought it would be an opportune time to have a break and give his furry friends some attention. The truck would be loaded later in the afternoon.

CH 61 – JOE –
ALICE DOESN'T LIVE HERE ANYMORE

1985

The gardener leant on his rake and watched as the old lady made her way across the freshly moved lawn. She moved like she was eighty or more, but he realised she was probably a lot younger than that. He'd seen how some of the meds they dished out did this sort of thing. The woman's limbs were as rigid as steel girders, and yet with each step her body shook like jelly.

Years ago, more than ten he thought, she had a friend that used to come and visit her every few weeks. Not that the lady with the stick always noticed. Her friend was a wiry wisp of a woman. She used to walk with her, talk with her, sit with her. Sometimes her visitor helped her look for her little boy, that's what she used to mumble, 'I want to find my baby boy.' Prodding under bushes. Behind trees. Under cricket kits. She never found him. Then the wispy lady never came back. Maybe she'd put up with her robotic companion long enough. The lady with the stick. The lady with the coiled snake of a scar sliced into her forehead. She'd been at the asylum for more than thirty years. For a lot of that time, she'd been heavily medicated. Wandering. Seeking. The gardener knew her name. It was Alice. Sometimes she spoke to him. Sometimes the words made sense. Mostly they were jumbled. Then one day, and the next, and the next, she wasn't there.

He whispered to himself, 'Alice doesn't live here anymore.'

⋆

Joe had been called to Callan Park Hospital by Dr Jerome Cornelius, one of the senior administrators of the facility. Dr Cornelius had arranged for a private meeting to discuss the death of one of Joe's relatives. A colleague of Dr Cornelius had also been asked to attend the meeting. 'Mr Keneally, I believe you know Dr Hopgood well. He will assist me in what I about to tell you.'

The three of them sat at a small round table in the corner of the office. They were surrounded by wall-to-wall shelving stacked with folders containing hundreds of internee histories. Joe was expecting to hear about the death of a long-lost cousin or a great-aunt he didn't know he had. The news when it came left him speechless. He now understood why Hops had been called in.

A thick file was placed on the table. Inside the cover was a loose document. The death certificate. *Cause of death: Cerebrovascular accident, accompanied by haemorrhage.* Further on it read, *haemorrhagic stroke.* He examined the contents of the folder carefully, still trying to comprehend the revelation that his mother had been alive for all those years. So near to where he lived and worked. A universe away. The deception of the graveyard inscriptions struck him with the force of the slabs they'd been written upon. His father. Nan Winn. Their secret. Truths withheld for years.

He was still coming to grips with the decades-long history when Cornelius spoke. 'Your mother had been interned here at Callan Park following a lengthy stay at Balmain Hospital. As you can see, her history included self-harm and several instances of psychotic behaviour, including the physical abuse of her infant child. This being you.'

'I already know about the mental breakdown and the accident that followed. I've heard the story time and time again.' Joe paused, fighting back tears and the rising contents of his stomach. He recounted the story he'd been told. About the fall that resulted in her death.

'Joe, your father and grandmother must have thought it best not to tell you what really happened to your mother. Perhaps in the course of time they'd planned to convey the whole story. But then they both passed away and their secret remained a secret. Until now, of course.'

Dr Hopgood scrutinised Joe while he was being bombarded with the tragic family revelations. Up to this point, he seemed to be holding it together. But he wondered how long his friend's composure would last.

Dr Cornelius continued, 'She was registered here as Alice Hewitt. The only person who ever came to see her was listed as Winifred McCabe. It took us a long time to connect Alice Hewitt to you, and that was only by the chance discovery of a record from Gladesville Mental Hospital where your mother had received electric shock treatment. She had broken her ankle as a result of her convulsions. The doctor who treated her ankle listed her as Alice Keneally. In his records he had made note of self-inflicted wounds on her arms and torso. This prompted us to cross-check the names and connect the dots.'

Hopgood interrupted Cornelius to explain to Joe that all this additional information had come to light after his mother's body had been cremated. 'You must understand that without the presence of next of kin, this was standard practice. The ashes would then be scattered at various locations on the grounds of the asylum. All this new information about your mother's identity put a stop to that scenario.'

'We have retained her ashes for you.' Cornelius indicated the decorative box with the Callan Park insignia on the side of the package.

Joe turned quickly and excused himself. 'Sorry, I need to ...' He exited the room, leaving the heavy door open. The two doctors could hear the echo of his footsteps disappearing down the empty corridor.

Hopgood turned to his colleague. 'I'd better go and check on him.'

Hopgood's first stop was the staff washroom at the end of the corridor. The door was ajar, but no-one was inside. When he emerged from the foyer into daylight, Joe was seated on a sandstone wall, surveying the asylum's playing fields and the river beyond.

'I'm okay Hops. I'll work it out. I just needed to be out of that room and into a different space.'

Hopgood sat next to him without comment. They both looked in the direction of the loud, rhythmic chanting emanating from a nearby enclosure.

'What's going on there, Hops? What is it?'

'It's a game they play Joe. It's called *Man in the Middle*. And everyone gets a turn.'

CH 62 – JOE – THE ASHES

1985

I sat on the concrete siding staring across to Rodd Island. Behind me someone had picked up a rounded stone and skimmed it over the glassy surface of the river. It touched a good six times before its momentum ceased and it disappeared into the watery graveyard of Iron Cove.

I knew the gardener had been working close by, but it surprised me to see how he could have pitched the stone so well. Then I recognised who it was, and I was no longer surprised. He had always had a great arm. He grinned back at me because he knew he'd startled me. He'd been my hero back in my early teens. He'd been everyone's hero back in Nam. The dust-off man. The procurer for the *dust of life*. The saint.

'Alice doesn't live here anymore.' Those were the words he said to me right off the bat. How could he have known my thoughts? I embraced Steve Watson with all my despair, grief, affection.

I said to him, 'They never told me a thing Wotto. My father. Nan Winn. Not a word of truth. Now they're both gone.'

His answer came swiftly.

'How about a game of cricket, Joe? We can use some of the gear in the pavilion. I've got the keys. They let me look after all that stuff now.'

I was taken aback. I recognised the symptoms, but it didn't matter to either of us in the moment. I asked him if he wanted to bat or bowl.

'We should toss first. Heads I bat. Tails I bowl.'

He tossed. It came down heads.

'Okay. I bat. I'm Australia. You are England. We play for the Ashes.'

There was irony in the occasion since I'd just put my mother's ashes in the boot of my car.

Wotto hammered in the stumps and gave me a new six-stitcher. We played like we did when we were kids. Only this time it was on a proper pitch. He told me how he'd got rid of all the weeds by spraying it with herbicide. Then he planted the turf and rolled it. We played hard. Home conditions gave him an advantage for this particular match. But it was only the First Test. As usual, he took the opening lead. But we had more Test Matches to play. The Ashes were still up for grabs.

He showed me his scorebook. There was writing on every page. Over the top of the places for batsmen and bowlers. Over the top of the partnerships and progress scores. It told a muddled story of insanity and truth. I flicked through it.

*

I enter my name as the Reverend Watson. Head of the Church of Saints and Sinners. I am my family's benefactor. I fight for the little people, the pure of heart. I want to atone for what God the Father has done to us all. I am the dust-off man. There is a place for every-one in my Church.

*

My friends came to see me back then. They asked me if I had saved them all. I told them the war had saved them. Not I, not me. But then peace took them away. The Inattentive Lord doesn't care.

✳

Boris was my first nightmare. Preying on the dust. And Scotty made me chase the dragon. More Big H that I never needed. They shouldn't have been allowed to play the game. And then came Bluey, Superman, and Shrink. One day they will all turn into crystal. All into the same thing. Just like Balthus in Ballard's crystal book. They will all be taken in.

✳

I love my new truck. They gave it to me for my job. They let me drive all around the place. Pick up turf from one place and take it to another. Gardening here and there. Branches and weeds to the tip too. All around the place I drive. All the way to Canberra and back. And no-one ever knows.

✳

I miss Alice with the scar and the stick. She spoke to me sometimes. Mostly she babbled. One day she said she killed her mother. Another time she whispered she lost her baby boy. Who is to know if any of it is true.

✳

I couldn't read any-more. There was clarity there among the trickeries. Wotto's heroin addiction started back in Nam. And it looks like Scotty was one of his suppliers. His smile betrayed the effects of dehydration and addiction. His teeth were ring-barked. Some missing

224

entirely. Broken off at the gum. I guessed he was still on some kind of program, probably methadone. Band-aid therapy I thought. Like so many at the asylum.

I said goodbye to my friend from the past and promised I would return soon for the Second Test. 'Make sure the pitch takes spin,' I said. Wotto gave me the thumbs up. I drove back to Day Street in a state of confusion. There were too many things on my mind. My mother's ashes. Dot and Norm. Dot and Tom. Connor's health. Ken's rehab. My family's safety.

I sketched out what had happened to Margot. 'More details later,' I said. She wanted to comfort me then and there, but I wasn't ready for comforting. Not yet. I told her I was going to bury my mother. She knew where I was going.

*

I parked the car in Castle Street at the back border of the cemetery. St Patrick's was now heritage, so what I was about to do was theoretically illegal. Who was to know? It was already dark. The headlights from the cars on Pennant Hills Road and Church Street helped illuminate the gravestones just enough without me needing to use my torch. I'd thought clearly enough before leaving home to bring a garden trowel too. I didn't use it much at home. It reminded me of digging foxholes in Nam. Some of the memorials seemed familiar. I found the one that read, *Man is made by his beliefs* .... The rest was covered in moss. It was as if nature had hidden what I had to fill in for myself.

In the mist I stumbled on a tree root and dropped the container with the ashes into a nearby plot. Luckily the box held together. While trying to retrieve it, I cut my hand on a piece of broken glass. I was anxious and disoriented and had to use the torch I brought with me to find my way to the proper site. I removed the Callan Park insignia from the cremation vessel and replaced it with a smear of my own blood. I looked up and saw the familiar words. *Until we meet again.* I was in the right place.

I crouched low to avoid being seen. I didn't want any passers-by thinking I was desecrating a headstone, or worse still, robbing a grave. My training instilled on me that it was good strategy to start digging whenever there was risk of attack. I dug with my fingers and trowel. The hole needed to be deep enough to make sure the container was well covered. I didn't want a curious dog or possum unearthing it. By the time I finished I was sweating and covered in dirt. It was done. *Until we meet again.*

*

I got back home by ten. The boys were in bed. Margot was reheating some minestrone soup from the night before. I had a shower to freshen up and sat down to unwind. The soap helped. The soup helped. Margot helped. She waited for me to open up. She absorbed everything I told her about the day. Without her, without the boys, without Hops, I don't know if I would have survived. My mother was where she needed to be. It foreshowed a sort of completion. I don't kid myself that we are all reunited in the afterlife, in some sort of orgasmic timeless party. But I believe there is a certain spirituality that transcends death and our understanding of it. I ponder over the stories of our First Nations people. What we call the Dreamtime stories. The past, the present, and the future fused together. They make just as much sense as the religious who-ha that addled my brain when I was growing up.

I remember nan Winn reading about the Rainbow Serpent. The cycle of the seasons. The giver and the taker of life. Creation and destruction. The protector of the Land and its People. Timeless. Uncreated.

*

I lay there watching Margot undress. Since she started going to Misha's she had slimmed down and toned up. She looked fabulous. I'd gone the other way. And because of this, and a variety of other reasons, I became nervous about the prospect of our lovemaking. I needn't have worried. She worked her lips and tongue down my body. I was tentative at first. Then I returned her kisses with a savagery that the day's pent-up emotions unleashed. I saw in Margot all that was good in humankind. Then I was somewhere else.

In the dark I saw villagers killed. Raped. Maimed. Friends dying in my arms. An old woman's mutilated face. A corpse. Ashes. Body bags. I screamed in horror as I came. Margot cried out too.

I kissed her gently. We lay in each other's arms until morning.

CH 63 – DOT – SPIRIT PLACE

Normally Dot wouldn't be at the Dental Hospital on a Saturday. It was a sunny December day, and she knew it would've been nice to be out picnicking on the Harbour foreshores – taking in the yachts as they trained for the Boxing Day Sydney-Hobart Classic. She was almost seven months pregnant, and the heat outside had already taken its toll on her energy. The air conditioning in her office was a godsend. Her apartment in Surry Hills had ceiling fans, but that wasn't enough. Furthermore, she wanted to finish the paper she'd been working on for the Australian Dental Journal. Something needed to be done about the dental health of Aboriginal children in the Northern Territory. She hoped her contribution would draw attention to the paucity of dental facilities in the area. Get it done now she thought, because the birth of her child would undoubtedly put a hold on her politicking, at least for a while.

Norm was not in the slightest bit thrilled about becoming a first-time father. The prospect had never been a priority. Far from it. He made sure his work commitments took him away for as long as possible from what he perceived, rightly or wrongly, to be Dot's emotional and physical ups and downs. This weekend he was staying at the Hyatt in Canberra, covering the Royal Commission into British atomic tests in Australia. Dot suspected the Royal Commission wasn't the only thing he was covering.

Dot was alone in her office finalising the conclusions of her paper when her waters broke. She realised it was way too early for this to happen. There were still another eight weeks before her baby was due. She felt fragile and afraid, but resilient enough to phone for an ambulance. She made her way out of her office to a place she wanted to be. The air in the lift and corridors seemed unbearably stuffy, but she thought it was her desperate condition that made it seem worse. The pain started to come in spasms. The contractions longer, stronger. Less time in-between.

She reached the sixth floor. From habit she scanned the title on the door before entering. In gold lettering it read Professor Thomas O'Leary, Head of Periodontics. The scent in the compact space was his. She was immediately comforted by its cool stillness. The floor in the corner of the tiny room was covered with journal reprints. These had been sorted into neat stacks, as was his custom. One for essential reading, another for perusal. Next to the stacks there was a separate table on which were countless clinical slides. Some of these had been mounted into pockets on plastic sleeves, others loaded into a carousel. The main desk was tidy, perhaps too tidy for any work in progress.

Dot nudged the office door fully open before propping herself against the desk. She had told the ambos where to come. It being the weekend, the hallway lights had been turned off. The desk lamp was the only light she needed. She was afraid for the new life she was about to bring into the world. If worse came to worse, this would be her own and her baby's *spirit-place*. She was anxious, but not panicky. Nonetheless, she could feel the forces of creation tearing at the flesh of her existence. She waited and hoped it wouldn't be too long before the ambulance arrived. The bleeding was heavy. She was growing weaker.

'Dr O'Leary, I'm sorry to call you so early. And on a Sunday too. But would it be possible for you to come to the hospital? Right away if you can. It's a matter of grave urgency. I can't say much more on the phone. Please come asap, sir. Your office is a bloody mess!'

'It's all right now, Dr O'Leary. The ambos, police, and doctor have come and gone hours ago. You can go in.' The hospital security guard ushered Tom into his office, making sure he avoided the worst spots in case he stained his clothes.

'Thanks Percy. Perhaps you could fill me in on what has happened?'

The two men surveyed the room. A bloodstained coat and cloth had been thrown in a bundle in the corner next to the filing cabinets. There was a large mass of clotted blood beneath the desk, and a smaller patch on the writing surface. The notes and slides had been neatly moved to the side. Tom's paraphernalia was otherwise untouched. He sensed there was a strange emptiness in the room.

'Do you know who it was?' Tom at first thought it could have been one of the weekend emergencies from the downstairs clinic who had found their way up to his office. He hardly ever locked it. Then again, there was far too much blood to come from an extraction socket.

'The police didn't let on, but I reckon it was a boong in need of solitude.'

'Why do you say that Perce?'

'Well sir, they found a baby abo. A fesus dumped on your desk. Or so the doc said. I couldn't help overhearing.'

'Foetus,' Tom corrected. He immediately realised what must have happened.

'Bloody amazing, these people. Doc told the officer it was mal-formed or something. Webbed feet. Funny shaped mouth and head.'

'Do you know which hospital they took the mother to?'

'Yeah. Pretty sure it was Royal Prince Alfred. The office won't be cleaned until Monday, sir.' Percy looked up to apologise for the delay, but Tom was gone.

CH 64 – COTTER – ART OF THE ASSASSIN

1985

The tinted windows allowed an attenuated stream of light into the hospital room. It was the middle of the day. The smell of disinfectant hovered in the air. Tom had been there overnight. He held Dot's hand. Neither spoke. No need. There was a small TV bracketed to the ceiling. The walls were bare apart from one piece of tinsel stuck with double-sided tape above the bed – a trifling reminder that Christmas Day had come and gone. There was another bed in the room too, but it was empty. Tom used it occasionally to get some rest. He'd been with Dot most of the time since her miscarriage. They watched the TV as the yachts, spinnakers set, made their way through the Heads and down the coast. It had been another perfect start to the Sydney-Hobart Yacht Race.

*

A string of advertisements followed – *Razzamatazz*, *Tab Cola*, *Mrs Marsh and the liquid gets in*, and finally *Madge and you're soaking in it*. Then there was a cross back to the TV newsroom for the top stories of the day.

Police believe the body of a man found yesterday in Cleveland

*

Four men and one woman assembled in the conference room at Sydney Police Headquarters.

Chief inspector Harold Cotter stood in front of a whiteboard, scribbling down the points he planned to discuss with his group of experts. Cotter was a no-nonsense veteran cop, with an impressive record of getting results. His appearance and demeanour were not unlike that of a certain well-known, polo-playing, media mogul. But there the similarities ended. Cotter had no time for sports entrepreneurship or other leisurely pursuits. His ultimate task in life was the policing of crime.

Also present at the meeting was uniformed senior sergeant Rex Baker – a by-the-book investigator, fastidious and loud. Across the table from Baker was chief forensic pathologist Dr Felicity Le Guin – tall, super intelligent, and a staunch ally of Cotter's, the man who had appointed her. Two specialists in military-related PTSD made up the five – medical psychiatrist Dr Gregory Hopgood and clinical psychologist Mr Joseph Keneally.

Chief inspector Cotter began, 'Good morning one and all. I've called you into Headquarters to help piece together what happened to these victims.' Everyone's eyes followed his.

Graphic photographs of the victims' bodies were pinned to mobile display panels adjacent the whiteboard. A nearby table housed labelled items pertinent to the murders.

'Apart from the two victims you see here on the left, there is also mystery surrounding the murder two years ago of a third person that has certain similarities to the other two. Photos of this case are on the adjacent board. Perhaps we should bracket all three together. I say that because I believe there are indications that all three murders, perhaps I should call two of them assassinations, were committed by a person or persons with a certain type of military training.' Hopgood's eyes widened marginally.

'Here's what we have. All three victims were stabbed by a double-edged commando style knife. You see on the table an example of such a weapon. This one is a British made Fairbairn-Sykes commando knife. In all three instances, the entry point was at the side of the neck. The thrust was deep beyond the midpoint. The knife was then ripped forward to sever the major blood vessels, the trachea, and the larynx. Death for all three would have been quick and silent. Initial forensic findings are as follows.'

'Mr Chen Lee, the first victim, was abandoned face-down as he fell. The entry point was on the left side of his neck. His right ear had been excised as a souvenir or message.'

'Mrs Linh Nguyen is not officially the second victim of the same assailant, but I believe she is. She was dispatched in a similar fashion. The initial stab was on the left. Her left ear was excised, and her body was dumped into a Vinnies clothing bin.'

'In the case of the third victim, Mr Randolph Saxe-Coburg, forensics have determined that the angle of the initial thrust was slightly different than Mr Lee's, indicating he may have been approached from the front so he could see his killer. The initial stab for him was also on the left side of his neck, like Mrs Nguyen and Mr Lee. This time, he was purposely positioned face-up, arms extended in the form of a cross. His right ear had been excised.'

'Over to you.' Cotter's gaze moved to momentarily single out each one of his specialist group. 'What do you make of all this?'

'Sounds to me like special forces training.' Joe started to speak before he was acknowledged. 'Perhaps working as an individual or for someone with a grievance or agenda. Mr Lee owned a gambling den, didn't he?'

Senior sergeant Rex Baker chimed in, 'Chen Lee was aspiring to do a lot more than oversee gambling, Mr Keneally. He also had visions of becoming a major drug importer and distributer. Almost certainly, he was eliminated at the order of a competitor. Back at the time of the first murder, Saxe-Coburg had worked for Lee as a procurer and bagman. But it seems since then he has been involved with an illicit drug trafficking business himself.'

Cotter continued, 'Now, about the woman Mrs Linh Nguyen. She seems clean. Husband, a well-respected medico. Mother of two. We think wrong place, wrong time. And yet, she still had her ear souvenired. Another indication of an ex-soldier? Or perhaps someone that wants us to think it was an ex-soldier?'

This time it was Hopgood's turn. 'Maybe collateral damage in the case of Mrs Nguyen. PTSD is a condition that can lead to triggered reactions associated with flashbacks of previous trauma. She was probably a victim of war, once or twice removed. I know for sure our guys didn't use that knife technique in training, but I also know a few of my patients, and Joe does too, I suspect, that were well versed in the art of the quick kill. It could be anyone with that sort of training. It doesn't have to be military.'

'How about the missing ears?' This time from Le Guin.

Joe looked tense. 'I'm ashamed to say it, but I have to admit that that sort of thing occasionally happened back in Vietnam. I saw it myself while I was over there on patrol. After a kill, for instance. A few of my patients confess they did it. And they regret it. The Yanks were worse. Of course, in the case of what is being presented in this investigation, inspector Cotter is right, it could have been done to bamboozle our thinking.'

'Dr Le Guin, it's your turn.' Chief inspector Cotter directed his attention to the forensic pathologist. 'I know you are wanting to say more. Go ahead.'

Dr Felicity Le Guin walked up to the whiteboard and sketched three head and neck outlines, complete with cross-sections and rudimentary external anatomy.

'Gentlemen. There are indications that the means of approach, the entry points, the exit wound topography, and the way the ears were excised suggest the possibility of two killers, or at the very least, an ambidextrous single killer. Here is my argument.'

'Chen Lee. Approached from behind. Right hand grasping victim's face. Left hand stab from left side. Strong slash forward. Victim face down. Right ear pulled taut. Left hand cut to excise ear.'

'Linh Nguyen. Initial stab left side. In this case the exit wound was also subtly different from Lee's, suggesting it may have been done from the front. The victim fell face down. Left ear pulled taut. Right hand cut to excise ear.'

'Randolph Saxe-Coburg. Approached from the front. Head pulled back with the left hand. Left side of neck entry stab. Strong pull forward. Exit wound similar to Linh Nguyen's. Victim positioned face up. Right ear pulled taut with left hand. Right hand cut to excise ear.'

'First victim killed by left-hander. Second and third victims possible right-hander. Unless the assailant is close to 50/50 ambidextrous, the slash forward and rip or pull backward require a good deal of force and accuracy to have been enacted so precisely as these have been.

And in my experience, there is more than a passing military skill involved in the killings.'

Joe had been thinking about Scotty boasting about his *paranza corta* skills with the folding stiletto. Scotty had even tried to tutor him in the art of the assassin. But as far as he knew, he was a left-hander, even to the point of not playing the bagpipes in the conventional way. Joe wondered if Scotty-come-Dino had become a two-handed assassin. He was ambidextrous enough when it came to how he held his can of beer after all.

Joe didn't say anything to Cotter. Not yet. He needed to talk to Hops first.

*

Dot wriggled into a sitting position in the hospital bed and turned to Tom. 'Maybe it's time for our afternoon siesta. Let's turn the TV off and ...'

We now have breaking news concerning new findings in the case of the 1977 killing of Griffith anti-drugs campaigner Donald Mackay, whose body has never been found. Our investigative journalist on the ground Norman Lindsay will have more to say on this case in a special report due to air early in the New Year. Stay tuned.

'Heard any more from Norm?'

'You already know about the first telephone call. He cried and said how sorry he was. But that was from Canberra just before he set off for the Riverina district. The same old story with this morning's call. He wants to be with me he says, but he's on a big story that won't go away. And he needs to do it now. Says he has a contact in Canberra who is terrified he will be the next victim. Says it's one of his secret sources from times gone by. He reckons the story will blow the lid off organised drug crime across the state. Maybe the entire eastern seaboard. Then he hung up. He knows you're here with me, Tom. And he knows you'll look after me. I shouldn't worry about him the way I do. But I do. Norm's obsessed. And he's treading on unsafe ground.'

CH 65 – JOE – THE SECOND TEST

I found Wotto raking leaves and branches from around the seats bordering the foreshore. Once he saw me he dropped his rake and sprinted over. 'Did you bring your cricket gear, Joe? Don't worry if you didn't. You can borrow from any of the kits I have in the shed. I've got all the keys.'

'I hope the pitch takes spin, Wotto. It's the only chance I have against your batsmen.'

'Don't worry, Joe. It's a four-day pitch. Slight cracking. A few bare patches. Perfect for your leggies. I bet it'll be a close contest. Remember, my Australian side is already one Test up. It's your job to see if England can draw level.'

This time I won the toss and decided to bat. Wotto had been working on an older ball he had in his kit. Rough one side, shiny on the other. I had trouble handling the reverse swing until he began to tire. My last wicket stand was a Test record. Still maybe not enough.

'You must have been practicing, Joe. It's my turn to bat after lunch.'

We ate the sandwiches Margot had prepared for us. Drank a couple of Fantas too.

While Wotto was loading leaves and branches onto the back of his truck I had another look through his scorebook. It was chockers to the last page.

"

*

The roses are beautiful. They are mine. They are blood red, and the thorns pierce the flesh like talons. They are beautiful, nonetheless. The grass, the trees, the bushes cover my domain. I make them grow. They blend with the ashes I scatter. And the seeds I sow.

*

I miss them all. My flock of dust. My mixed children. The boy never had a chance. Boris took his innocence one day. Scotty, his existence on another. I was too late. Into the water and left him there. I should have pitched them out of the Huey when I had the chance. I still watch them sometimes. Sometimes I toss a coin. Sometimes I flip a bat. Heads or tails. Hills or flats. Life or death.

*

Joe and I are mates. But not teammates. I am Australia from the left. Geoff Dymock. David Hookes. He is England from the right. Ian Botham. Graham Gooch. I will beat him on a crumbling pitch. Scoring quickly. Hit and run.

*

'Are you ready Joe? I need to quicken my run rate before there's an appeal against the light. Try your googly. I'm pretty sure I can pick it now. Quickly, quickly.'

I returned the scorebook to the cabin of the truck. The writing on the back cover caught my attention. It was new.

It's not their business to know.
Here and there I go.
I will take back what was stolen
Once I make the roses grow.

And then, under it, another poem ...

Come take this half soul,
The final floating dreams
Of a poor man's love,
His spasm flight is flown,
And puckered with his sad remains,
Hovering with unblushed skin
Above the shore.

They were pearls of purity
Or ruby fire,
They were the dust
For whom the night now weeps,
More so than I have longed
For their right to sleep,
Amid rainbow shadows when they die.

*

I remember Wotto used to read poetry back in Nam. His favourites were Samuel Taylor Coleridge and Gerard Manley Hopkins. Drugs and religion. A dangerous mix.

✳

'I win, Joe. But it was closer this time. Lucky for me I can pick your flipper. Maybe next time you need to bowl some offies.'

✳

Margot played with her glass of wine. 'Joe, it has to be Superman. He's not at rehab anymore. And the only things that remain in the storage unit are the *Superman Removals* sidings. The truck is gone. Think about it, Joe. Number one: Chen Lee ran the gambling house where Viktor gambled away Ken's money. Number two: You said he told you he had something he had to do the same day that Vietnamese woman was killed at the Birkenhead carpark. Number three: Randolph. You remember he stayed for a while at my place. Maybe it was drugs and not sex those people lined up for. And he turned out to be Viktor's lover. Let's face it, Ken had motive to kill all three.'

'How about the knife skills and the left- and right-hand scenarios for the assailant?'

'Joe. You were the one who told me that Ken can throw a ball or a grenade with either arm. And Scotty kept sparring with him with that Sicilian knife thing.'

'You mean the *paranza corta* knife fighting? But that was with a folding stiletto. These people were killed with a commando knife.'

'Same kind of thing.'

'Couldn't it just as easily have been someone else? Scotty, for instance?'

'You know it couldn't have been him. You told me yourself he had iron-clad alibis at the time of all the murders.'

'That's what concerns me, Margot. It's all too organised and watertight. It doesn't add up. Scotty or Mr Dino could have killed all three victims too. Anyway, I've seen Scotty whip an ear off with his right hand. He had quite a collection in his sporran. Stunk the place out. And it seems Scotty was supplying drugs to some of the troops back in Nam. Wotto's scorebook laid it out in a garbled fashion. And heroin did Wotto in. I can't even get Bluey's opinion anymore. He's too dodgy to trust. I think he knows a lot more than what he lets on.'

'Let's give it a rest, Joe. How about we go visit Dot again? She gets back home on Thursday. I'll make her room look nice and welcoming.'

'You obviously don't know the latest, my sweet. Dot's moving in with Tom.'

*

Joe sat out on the veranda and gazed at the skiffs on the river. Then beyond them to Callan Park. He'd been through it all. Experienced it all. Sense and sensibility. Pleasure and pain. He flicked through some of the science fiction books he'd borrowed from Superman and came upon a familiar story – Bester's *Fondly Fahrenheit*. Ken had underlined some of the text.

He doesn't know which of us I am these days, but they know one truth. You must own nothing but yourself. You must make your own life, live your own life, and die your own death – or else you will die another's.

Then he opened the *Elric Saga* by Moorcock. Another underlined section.

Elric knew that everything that existed had its opposite. In danger he might find peace. And yet, of course, in peace there was danger. Being an imperfect creature in an imperfect world he would always know paradox.

Joe closed the book and wondered what would happen next.

CH 66 – JOE – BEHOLD THE MAN

Hops and I got the call two days before the end of the year. Neither of us had planned anything special for the holidays, but the prospect of attending an actual murder scene had never crossed our minds.

We were picked up from our respective residences and escorted to the airport. The chartered flight included all the participants of our recent meeting at police headquarters, as well as several other official-looking uniformed personnel and various auxiliary staffers from the investigative and forensic teams.

Thirty minutes after take-off, we were landing at Canberra Airport. Another thirty or so minutes and we were pulling up at the Ainslie house. The property had already been cordoned off as a crime scene, but the local constabulary had been cautioned that the investigation would be conducted by the Sydney-based homicide division. Chief inspector Cotter was an imposing figure as he alighted from the police transport vehicle, and it would seem that his reputation had preceded him. No-one was going to argue with his directives.

Hops and I were ushered into a tent that had been set up in the front yard. We were ordered to dress in the appropriate clothing, which included a full body suit with hood, a mask, overshoes, and gloves. We'd been told by the homicide team that our expertise would be highly valued, but we were also well aware that we'd be carefully watched in case we contaminated any useful evidence.

Sergeant Baker and Dr Felicity Le Guin led us into the central hall of the house. On the way in, I almost tripped on a bowl of water that had been left on the deck. I later learned it was the golden retrievers from next door that had raised the alarm. They kept barking until their owners became suspicious and called the police. I could still hear them woofing from inside the neighbours' house. They obviously would have liked to have been a part of the nearby ruckus. It was quite the opposite for the cat on the roof of the backyard shed. Basking in the sun. Oblivious to all the comings and goings of the authorities and the media.

The first room we passed was crammed with stacks of books, mostly science fiction paperbacks. No prizes for guessing who that room belonged to. The room was dusty and looked as though it hadn't been used for quite some time. There were a couple of posters I could see on the wall facing the doorway. One of them showed a human-like robot staring out across rice fields to an orange sky. The other poster appeared religious. It was headed *Behold the Man*. It depicted Jesus being crucified. In the background was something that looked like a huge broken egg. The face of Jesus had been covered by an edited snapshot of someone else.

I will never forget what I saw in the next room. It was the actuality of the poster I'd seen in Superman's room. The mutilated body had been nailed to the wall. The face was the same face that had been pasted onto the poster. The re-creation was unmistakable, except the man's throat had been opened to the point just short of decapitation. It was Viktor Karlikov. Ken had shown me several photos of him during our therapy sessions. I felt sick, but not as sick as Hops who needed to excuse himself to get some fresh air.

I briefly told Dr Le Guin about the sessions at my clinic – about

Ken's predilection for science fiction, and his more recent stint in rehab. In return, she discussed her initial thoughts with me. We stood and looked down at the bloodied desk.

'The victim had been working here when he was approached from behind. He was slain while seated. Initial thrust from the left. Slashed forward just like Chen Lee, only jagged and deeper, nowhere near as clean as any of the others. One ear gone. A neat excision this time. Victim instantly dead. Pooled blood on the desk. Interestingly, the blood had dried before he was moved. I'd say he was transferred to the wall several hours after he was murdered.'

'Wouldn't that be unusual for the murderer to wait so long before moving him?'

'Yes Mr Keneally, quite unusual. But who is to say how the mind of a murderer works?'

*

Outside it had started to sprinkle. One of the police attending the boundary tape was voicing his thoughts on Canberra weather to his colleague, 'Typical ACT summer. It's done this the last few days. None of us begrudge a little rain when it's hot. Just never enough to make the grass green.'

Cotter overheard what was said as he was making his way to the tent to remove his disposable suit. It prompted him to scrutinise the driveway. Distinct grooves were imprinted into the partially dry clay at the side of the concrete. He motioned to one of his team to follow up on his observation. 'At least two large vehicles have been in here recently. Different types of tread too. Let's get a few photographs and casts before it gets any wetter.'

*

Ken had driven up the driveway on the day of days, hoping against hope his homecoming would be welcomed. In some remote part of his brain, he imagined Viktor coming out to greet him, just as he had done in the past. Remembering all the good times they shared. Forgetting Essie altogether.

Instead, he was met by Abbott and Costello, eager for attention. He gave each of them a rub and a pat, forever yearning for a belated appearance from Viktor.

He scanned the length and breadth of the backyard. It looked unexpectedly well kept. His prized roses had been cared for too. He wondered if Viktor had done all this for him, hoping one day he would return.

He entered the house through the sliding door of the terrace. Moved silently down the hallway as he'd done a thousand times before. Ready to console. Ready to offer sympathy and love. He stopped abruptly at the doorway of the study. His onetime lover was face down on his desk. His throat had been ripped open like a beast at a pagan festival.

He knew immediately who had done it. The desk calendar confirmed it – the Sicilian assassin.

'Run Plan-B by Dino'
'Pick up laundry'
'Gardening'

On the flip page for the following day, just one word ...

'Blue'

He tore out both pages, folded them and put them in his pocket. *Plan-B* had to be something to do with Bluey.

✳

Ken loved Viktor like fervent believers love their god. He lifted him from his place at the desk and clothed him in his favourite purple robe. Then he went outside to the shed to get garden shears, a hammer, and some nails. Just as described in *John 19*, he wove a makeshift crown of thorns from the rose bushes. Placed the crown on Viktor's head. Moved him over to the wall and nailed him to an imaginary cross. *Behold the Man*. He knelt at Viktor's feet and gave thanks to the man who was at once his Man and his God. He apologised as he excised one of Viktor's ears. Dipped the blade into a pool of his former lover's blood, then wiped it, making sure some of the residue remained. To gain final absolution there was one more thing he had to do. And so, despite his despair and his grief, the man once known as Superman hatched a plan.

✳

Ken made his way to Sydney in a state of numb detachment. He couldn't remember the details of the drive back, apart from stopping once near Bargo to fill up. He'd been too late to save his beautiful Viktor. Now it was time for revenge.

Next day he parked his truck a good hundred metres from *The Sicilian* down Gipps Street. It was 2am on December 31st. The street was empty, but the roar from the gusty summer wind made it seem as though there was more happening than there really was. He checked the code lock at the side security gate, hoping the key numbers hadn't changed since the time of their hoochie reunion. He remembered Scotty's favourite roulette habits, always favouring the prime numbers. He entered 2, 3, 5, 7. The shackle came free silently, and he entered the backyard without incident. The streetlights gave just enough illumination for the next part of his plan.

He had two plastic boxes with him. The type he knew the restaurant used. He buried one of the containers in the corner of the garden.

The next part of the plan was going to be tricky. There was a freezer box inside the downstairs laundry. Another digital lock. He tried the same four number code. Nothing. Then he entered it backwards like they used to do at Vungers. Numbers 7, 5, 3, 2. The shackle loosened. Ken entered. Closed the door and switched on the torch.

He retrieved the two pages of Viktor's desk calendar from his pocket. Scrunched them up and threw them in a nearby wastebin.

The restaurant's freezer, itself, was formidable. One of those industrial types, with a large lid that swung upward. The top layer was crammed with smaller items. Sausages, mince, fish. He lifted this layer out and placed it on the bench. The next tier had larger items. Shoulders, ribs, legs of lamb, whole chickens. He nestled the second plastic box under the curved section of the ribs. The top layer was replaced. Lid closed. Torch out. Door closed. Lock fastened. Side gate shut. Locked again.

He'd done it all. Now it was time to drop an anonymous tip to Mr Exclusive. Dino had it coming. And it would hurt.

*

Ken had been clean for months. The stress of the last few days had driven him to rethink his options for celebration. Maybe just a few lines for the road. He still had a stash for such an occasion.

The cocaine kicked in harder and quicker than he had anticipated. Probably because he'd been drug free for so long. Coming down the hill, he clipped the side of the gutter as he was steering into the cross street. The truck jack-knifed and rolled onto its side. The front window shattered, and he was showered with splinters of glass. It didn't take long before the police arrived.

CH 67 – KEN – THE RAINBOW SERPENT

Ken had been searched, stripped of any possessions, and unceremoniously thrown into the local lockup. His erratic behaviour at the time of arrest had subsided to some extent, but his pupils were still dilated, and his heart pumped like he'd just run back-to-back 400-metre sprints.

He sat in the corner of the cell, head in hands. Blood oozed through his outstretched fingers. Nightmares of the last week came flooding back to him, blending with memories of Vietnam and the after-effects of cocaine and alcohol. He had lost his lover twice. Once to Saxe-Coburg. And again, horrifically to the Ndrangheta. Revenge was only part-way done. Dino would get his just deserts soon enough.

He wrenched himself up, leaned against the nearest wall and started to draw. With his finger wet with his own blood he sketched a giant 'S', similar in shape to the tattoo he sported on his chest. Then he turned the 'S' into a snake. Triangular head on top. Tapered body and tail below. The bleeding from his forehead gave no sign of stopping, and so he continued to insert evenly spaced bands along the length of the snake's body. In the dim light, the serpent seemed to move in unison with the shadow of the artist's arm. Ken's time in the Territory's rehabilitation unit had not escaped the impact of the Land and its stories. His creation was now a Rainbow Serpent. The red striations were those of summer. He and the snake were one. The giver of life itself. And at the same time, the vengeful entity that could just as easily take life away.

In all of this, Ken's rib cage had been jerking in fits and starts. Now it mechanically eased as the effects of the cocaine dwindled. Without notice, there was a metallic clunk, an unlocking of the prison door. The attending constable entered with resolute trepidation. 'The doctor is here to check you out, Mr Campbell. He has an associate with him who says he knows you.'

'Hi Joe. Hi Hops. I stuffed up, didn't I?'

'Let me have a look at those cuts. I've brought my medical kit with me. Don't use it much these days, but it's good to have in case of emergency. I'll clean you up and give you the once over. But we'll need to move you to a room with better hygiene. You're not going to jump me and escape, are you?' They laughed. It eased the tension.

Half an hour later Hopgood had tidied Ken's face, placed a few steri-strips, and made sure he wasn't concussed.

'Good as new, mate. No more of that coke stuff. Got it?'

'I was stupid, Joe. The Canberra thing stressed me out big time. I'm guessing you know about that.'

'Yes Ken. We were there. I'm sorry about Viktor. I know you still loved him. He got mixed up in some shifty business. The police are going to need to interview you, and you'll have to explain a few things about why you returned to the house when you did, and what you did while you were there. All in good time. You'll be moved to more comfortable quarters soon enough. In the meantime, you're going to have to stay here. Enjoy! Oh, and I have a couple of Subway footlongs and juice for you. The constable has checked them out. No kryptonite.'

'Funny bastard! Thanks Joe. Thanks Hops. You are my mates. I'll pay you back I promise. I've been let down by some of the others. But what goes around comes around. All I have to do is wait.' Joe wondered what he meant by that. Maybe it was a good time to find out.

'You both off now?'

Joe winked at Hopgood. 'Hops has another call to make. I'm staying behind to fine dine with you. It's okay with the constable. I got two lots, didn't I? Which one do you want? Chicken teriyaki or meatballs? Can't have you eating alone, can I?'

Hopgood knew what Joe was up to. The young constable had no objections, provided the cell was kept locked until it was time for Joe to leave.

*

Several groups of New Year's Eve revellers were at *The Sicilian* that night. The first-floor terrace was the perfect place for patrons to view the fireworks above Five Dock Bay. Dino was a happy man. His satisfaction came not so much from the success of the fireworks display, but from the knowledge his restaurant had raked in more money on that one evening than it had ever done before. Paulo the maître d' had been the perfect host, and Marco the head chef had done the establishment proud. Now it was time to clean up and hit the sack.

Dino sent his staff home once the main chores had been done. It was almost 3am, and all he had to do was put the bins out for collection. He dragged all seven out the side exit. Then, one-by-one, he wheeled them around to Lyons Road where the garbage truck would empty them in a few hours. By the time the final bin was positioned Dino felt he'd earned a good eight hours kip. He looked across at the deserted road, realising that most of this evening's customers were already comfortably asleep in their beds. He looked again and noticed a truck pull out from its parked position a short distance down the road, its occupants silhouetted against the glow of the streetlights. He was about to warn the driver he'd forgotten to turn on his headlights. That was before the truck mounted the curb and accelerated along the footpath towards him.

✶

Driver and passenger felt the impact. Heard the bins being scattered. Sensed something soft being dragged under the chassis. Then a jolt, and they were back on the road. They looked at each other and nodded. The truck continued along Lyons Road for another kilometre before chucking a U-ie and returning to the grounds of Callan Park.

First light on the first day of the year revealed a brand-new score-book on the truck's front seat.

In spidery script on the open first page –

Toss a coin. Flip a bat. Life or death.

Underneath it in classical style –

As I believe, so I am.

CH 68 – COTTER – THE WRAP UP

1986

A week later the same five people were called into police headquarters. This time chief inspector Cotter sat at the end of a long conference table. No whiteboard was needed.

'No doubt you have all heard about the hit and run outside *The Sicilian* restaurant on the morning of New Year's Day. Not a single witness has come forward. Instead, we received a tip-off from an investigative reporter, one you may already know about given his high public profile. He claims his source was anonymous, and at this stage I'm willing to believe him. Anyway, the tip-off came at a price. The price tag includes granting him an exclusive story about the serial murders we've been investigating. The possible link these murders have to organised crime – and I include the killing of Lombardino in this – is more contentious, and I am still considering whether this particular reporter will be permitted to include that part of the story in his article.

'Senior sergeant Baker justifiably objected to granting any privileges to the reporter, and I was in two minds myself regarding the decision. Ultimately, however, the information we have since received has proven accurate. What you are going to be told today remains strictly confidential until the time is right to release it to the public. At this stage, the reporter in question has been prohibited from publishing his story, subject to my approval. I believe a certain amount of censorship will be required. I haven't broached this subject with him until I give it further thought.

'I will now leave it to senior sergeant Baker to fill you in on the investigation.'

*

Don Giuseppe Roccella, comfortably dressed in his favourite cardigan and loafers, sat across from Norman Lindsay at *Il Culinario*. It was just the two of them. Outside, Roccella's henchmen stood at the door.

'Mr Lindsay, I believe the Ndrangheta have been more than helpful to you in your career. Would you agree?' Norm nodded. 'We have given you material leads where none existed for your media colleagues – or should I say, your competition. Admittedly, you helped us too. It was a legitimate way of undermining the interests of our business rivals through trustworthy media sources. Win-win. But recently, you took it upon yourself to turn your head in our direction. This was not a wise move, considering all we have done for you. The hand that feeds you should never be bitten. We provided you with information and opportunities which, combined with your considerable talents, took you to the top echelon of your profession. But surely you must know by now that when you reach for the stars you must first have your feet planted firmly on the ground. Our mutual friend Mr Lombardino forgot about this principle. So too did Lee and the others.'

Norm sat there with downcast eyes. Sweating. He couldn't bring himself to utter a sound until he'd heard more of what Roccella had to say.

'Very few people should ever know the whole truth. Please understand. It confuses the main issues that need to be resolved. You should never underestimate the power of those that manage what you see and what you don't see. Your proposed interview with Mr Karlikov was ill conceived. Frankly Mr Lindsay, you are lucky to be alive.

'I will now tell you what truths I have uncovered so far. Then I will tell you what you are permitted to say. My truths and your truths will not be the same. That is the way of the world.

'And by the way Mr Lindsay, in the next few days you will receive a job offer from the British Broadcasting Corporation. You will accept it and resign from all your current means of employment in this country. All your stories from now on will be vetted. This offer is non-negotiable. You will leave Australia and not return until I say. There will be consequences if you refuse any of these conditions. I'm sure you know what those consequences will be.'

CH 69 – JOE – WOULD IT CHANGE ANYTHING?

1986

Senior sergeant Baker started off by commending his team of investigators and ancillary staff. About the maxim that crime does not pay. About the mission of the police to bring evil to justice. While he was doing this my concentration wavered. I started thinking of Superman and his take on Michael Moorcock's concept of the multiverse. And I imagined how it would be in a parallel universe. One without war. One without peacetime tragedy. One in which Scotty, Superman, Bluey, and Boris were different. One in which Wotto, the Dreamer, and I were different too. In the reality I was now in I knew more than anyone else in the room. I could tell them every detail of how it all went down. But then again, I'm not sure it would change anything. Anything important, that is. The Ashes had already been won and lost, and it was time to move on.

*

When Baker started his pitch on Scotty, I switched on again. He described Alberto 'Dino' Lombardino as the manager and part-owner of *The Sicilian* restaurant. He believed his killing was targeted and was undoubtedly linked to organised crime. He called it a *reckoning*.

He then outlined what he and his team had discovered as a result of the tip-off. 'We unearthed a plastic box in the garden containing a double-edged commando knife, almost identical to the Fairbairn-Sykes one displayed at our first meeting. Forensics have examined traces of blood on the knife, and Dr Le Guin will let you know what pathology found. Furthermore, in a downstairs freezer we discovered another plastic box of similar description containing individually wrapped human ears. Once again, Dr Le Guin will tell you more about these rather distinctive morsels of skin and cartilage.'

Baker droned on for a few more minutes, and I confess my concentration waned again. Lack of sleep, I guess. I imagined I was at a park playing cricket with Wotto. This time we were both on the same side.

Then I snapped back to attention when it was Le Guin's turn.

∗

Felicity Le Guin remained seated at the table, her notes spread out before her.

'First of all, I will tell you what was found at Mr Lombardino's property. The plastic boxes – one in the garden, one in the freezer – were consistent with the same type of containers used at the restaurant to store food. No usable fingerprints were found on either one. The prints lifted off Mr Lombardino, as expected, were all over the lid of the freezer. Other prints were there too of course. Those of the staff.

'The traces of blood found on the knife were of two types. One was B positive. Approximately 8% of the population has this type. Mr Saxe-Coburg's blood type was B positive. The other blood type was O negative. Approximately 6% of the population has this blood type. Mr Karlikov's blood type was O negative.

'Now to the box of human ears found in the freezer. One of the ears was a clear match with Linh Nguyen. Another was a match for

Saxe-Coburg. Mr Karlikov's ear was there too. I'm sad to say there were more packages, but the contents of those had deteriorated to the point where any attempt to ID them would have been unreliable.'

I had to ask. 'How did the anonymous informer know about the plastic boxes and their contents?'

'We have considered that issue, Mr Keneally. The answer is, we don't know for sure. However, senior sergeant Baker may give you some insight into a possible answer.'

Baker was only too happy to chime in again. 'It is true. We may never find out the whole story. But we now believe Mr Paulo Luca – the assistant manager of *The Sicilian* – may have been our informer. Of course, we have no proof of this. I personally suspect he may have planted the incriminating evidence as well. However, Dr Le Guin and chief inspector Cotter disagree with me on this. Either way, we did discover that Paulo's full name is Paulo Luca Roccella. He is almost certainly a member of the Ndrangheta. Perhaps even the nephew of one of the head-honchos. That crowd do not tolerate discord. Alberto Lombardino transgressed. So too did Lee, Saxe-Coburg, and Karlikov. All of them lined their own pockets, while attempting to appear loyal to their benefactors. Over to you again Dr Le Guin.'

'In view of what we now know, the M.O. of the killings can now be based on concrete evidence, rather than speculation.' Le Guin gave a passing glance in Cotter's direction, then continued to scan her notes. 'Earlier on in the investigation we had to look at all possibilities.'

I noticed the suggestion of a smile on chief inspector Cotter's face. We all knew Cotter wanted to be seen to have got his man. I gave Hops a nudge. The rest of Le Guin's conclusions came as no surprise.

'This is what we know. All four cases, Chen Lee, Linh Nguyen, Randolph Saxe-Coburg, and Viktor Karlikov had similar if not identical knife wounds. Absence of other injuries indicates all were taken by surprise. All entry points were on the left side of the neck. All had one ear excised. Whether it was left or right depended on the approach of the assailant, rather than the position of the body.'

'We know Mr Lombardino was proficient at the Sicilian art of *paranza corta*, a style of knife fighting. He was a trained soldier and was in the habit of souveniring ears off the deceased in Vietnam. I believe Mr Keneally and Dr Hopgood can corroborate that. He was also left-handed. Furthermore, our search of his wardrobe found a pair of dark trousers with golden retriever fur on them. In addition to all that, a waste bin near the restaurant's freezer contained incriminating text from Mr Karlikov's desktop calendar.'

Senior sergeant Baker wanted to make his point. 'We now have evidence that Lombardino, Karlikov, and Saxe-Coburg were in the business of drug importation and distribution. Some of their operations appear to have been outside the structure of a certain organisation that shall go unnamed.'

'Thank you, senior sergeant Baker. I was getting to that.' Le Guin didn't appreciate the interruption.

'Don't make it sound like a Le Carré spy novel, Rex, just let Dr Le Guin finish what she wants to say. That should be enough.' Cotter was getting irritated by Baker's theatrics.'

'Anyway,' Le Guin continued, 'Lombardino was run down by a large vehicle that had mounted the curb outside his restaurant as he was putting out the garbage for collection. He had been dragged approximately a hundred metres down the road before his body was disengaged from the truck's undercarriage. He was dead at the scene. You must realise, some of his clothing had been ripped to shreds. Tyre marks on the victim's torso, as well as the tracking on the footpath, were those of a small truck, consistent with the gauge and tread pattern found in the driveway of the Ainslie house. This line of investigation, however, quickly headed for a dead-end. Several of the casual couriers employed by Karlikov for his computer business use a delivery vehicle of similar size, chassis, and wheel substructure. All these couriers have iron-clad alibis for the day of the murder.'

'Where does Ken Campbell and his truck fit into all of this?' I wanted to clarify the status of my friend and patient.

'I can answer that one for you, Mr Keneally.' Cotter looked like he wanted to round the meeting up before too much discord ensued. I could clearly see senior sergeant Baker wanted to add to the discussion. He was wriggling around like he was sitting on a red-hot poker. But this time he remained silent.

'Campbell did not kill Karlikov. We have witnesses that locate his truck a good deal short of Canberra at the same time Karlikov was killed. Campbell did, however, move and reposition the body after the event. This could be construed as interfering with the investigation. Then again, this was not done with malice or any attempt to deceive. Karlikov had been his lover, and I accept the fact that Campbell was distraught, resulting in his irrational behaviour. If I am to believe what you two gentlemen have told me,' he nodded to me and Hops, 'Campbell's gesture was done as an act of love, perhaps even adoration. He has after all been a voluntary patient of Mr Keneally's. And prior to the incident in Canberra, he had been at a rehabilitation centre in the Northern Territory. This facility had apparently helped him withdraw from his drug habit, as well as providing a good deal of protection to his whereabouts, in case he may have been located by those who wished him harm. It also stands that he is unlikely to have known about his part in the transportation of drugs in and around Canberra, and from one city to another. All other elements of his *Superman Removals* business have been checked and have been found to be above board.'

'In addition, it is likely Mr Campbell's return to cocaine contributed to the accident with his truck. And I believe you two gentlemen tended to his facial cuts and scrapes. Importantly, Campbell was in detention when Lombardino met his fate. His truck had been impounded at the same time. There is no suggestion that Campbell needs to be indicted for any of this. Perhaps another period of rehabilitation and community service would be in order, and I will trust that this proceeds with the supervision of you two gentlemen.'

Cotter then stood, bent slightly, and placed both his hands on the desk. He stared intently at all of us. Baker especially. 'I believe this case can be wrapped up. I shall now decide what news gets released to the public. You may all go home and enjoy some well-earned down-time.'

*

Chief inspector Cotter and Don Giuseppe Roccella met at a designated location under a banner of secrecy that would have done MI6 proud. Together, they made sure Norman Lindsay's exclusive article had been changed adequately enough to satisfy both parties before its public release. The police investigation had been praised for hunting down the serial killer. Gambling and illicit drug trafficking had been found to be the main reasons behind the killings. The article emphasised that Mrs Linh Nguyen had been an innocent bystander at the scene of a drug deal. The names Ndrangheta, Honoured Society, and Mafia were never mentioned in the article.

In a separate news item, the police expressed their indebtedness to the prudent approach taken by Mr Norman Lindsay, the investigative journalist responsible for uncovering a series of links between the murders. Mr Lindsay modestly commented that media integrity and its cooperation with law enforcement authorities provided the backbone of news coverage of the highest calibre. Following on from this he solemnly vowed to uphold the honour of his profession in his newly appointed position at the London office of the BBC.

CH 70 – JOE – WELCOME HOME

A still common depiction of the veteran is the potential violent, anti-social and depressed figure, alienated from the rest of the community and deeply angry towards it. The image, of course, had been rejected by the veterans themselves. Nevertheless, it has been extremely difficult for many veterans to live with, and in many ways, even harder to live down … A symbolic welcome may still fall short of the substantive rehabilitation many veterans expect. Nevertheless, sympathy to their needs among the wider community is essential … Today's welcome then will be more genuine and important if it encourages a continuing process of reconciliation within the community.

Sydney Morning Herald, Saturday 3rd October 1987.

*

I placed one foot in front of the other, this time less gingerly than I had the first time in-country. My legs were no longer jelly. I kept up with the others – side, front, and rear. My limp was barely noticeable. And the beret held my thinning hair firmly down in place to hide the scarring around my ear. I can laugh about it now.

As we paraded past the Town Hall I gave an eyes-right, and I swear I saw Harry 'the Dreamer' Russell grinning at me. I just wish Scotty, Bluey, Superman, and Wotto were here with me on this day. Just the way they had been back then.

I looked across at the crowd lining George Street. I saw Margot with her split-watermelon smile. Tears rolling down her cheeks. Connor and Richie yelling and waving their miniature flags.

'*Because I keep telling myself that everything will turn out all right,*' the Dreamer's words whispered back to me.

The piper stood on the official platform playing Waltzing Matilda. It could have easily been Scotty piping away. Like he'd done at the Dat.

Then the bugle. The Last Post. And the words from Binyon's poem:

They shall not grow old, as we that are left grow old:
Age shall not weary them, nor the years condemn.
At the going down of the sun and in the morning
We shall remember them.

*

Then I saw my sister Dot. Tom stood behind her, arms around her. She held two flags: the official Australian flag with the Union Jack, the Commonwealth Star, and the Southern Cross. And the Aboriginal flag, its top half black representing the Aboriginal People, the lower half red, standing for the earth and the colour of ochre, and the circle of yellow in the centre representing the sun. She held it for all First Nations People. She held it for Norman 'Bluey' Lindsay. Black, red, and yellow. But no Blue.

*

*This was an emotional purging of anger, frustration, bitterness,
confusion, and rejection, which has possessed these men since they
returned from that terrible Asian war. The personal agonies of these
men are hard to understand for those who were not there, but the
statistics are shocking. Twice as many have died since they returned,
as were killed in the war. Hundreds have committed suicide.*
Sydney Morning Herald, Sunday 4th October 1987.

✳

Ken Campbell watched the Welcome Home Parade on the TV of his
rented Kings Cross apartment. He then retired to his bedroom and
swallowed the contents of two packets of Oxycodone, washed down
with a bottle of vodka. Drained of the life he once had, he lay down
to die. He mouthed familiar words before losing consciousness.

*'You must own nothing but yourself. You must make your own life,
live your own life, and die your own death – or else you will die
another's.'*

Superman was discovered several weeks later. There had been a complaint about the smell.

CH 71 – JOE – BLUE EYES ON BLUE

We were in Darwin to attend my sister's NAIDOC Award Ceremony. Many believe she will be in the running for an Order of Australia one day. I hope so. Margot, the boys, and I arrived a couple of days early so we could see the sights of Kakadu. And today, we're doing some retail therapy at the Mindil Beach Markets. I looked between the bobbing heads of my fellow shoppers as Richie and Connor meandered along the beach, silhouettes vibrating against the setting sun and the rippling sea. Connor had grown so much, it was impossible to work out who was who. Margot and I browsed the stalls looking for some handcrafted gifts and artwork, mindful we'd been warned by Dot not to buy anything too expensive without her advice.

*

'It was Dr Dorothy O'Leary's brainchild.' That's how the Chief Minister of the Northern Territory described it. My sister's original idea was to deliver dental care through primary school clinics. The first ones were at Braitling, Gillen, and Tennant Creek. Then her concept escalated. She didn't stop with dental services, she also started to lobby for funds to make medical services available to the broader First Nations population by planning community clinics across the more remote parts of the Territory. Dot is making a difference! And today's ceremony is honouring her contribution as the instigator and head of the whole project.

We sat there next to Tom for the presentation. Dot gave her acceptance speech and mingled among the dignitaries before finally inching her way to us. I love Tom like a brother. He's the best man I could have ever hoped for Dot. He resigned his university position to support her. And now he ventures out in his four-wheel drive with his mobile surgery trailing along. Going to out-of-the-way settlements. Delivering dental services where it would never have been thought possible.

I gave my little sister a gentle hug, and asked her how she was feeling. She smiled at me like she always does.

'All is good Joe. Eight months now, and she or he is kicking like a hip-hop dancer.'

I teased her when she admitted she didn't know if it was a boy or a girl.

'I don't want to know, Joe. It's going to be a surprise.'

I asked if she had decided on names. Up until then she hadn't let on, not even to Margot.

'If it's a boy, I'll call him Sydney. If it's a girl, Katherine.'

The twinkle in her eyes teared up again.

'There's something I want to tell you, Joe. Something about *us*. Tom found out after one of his outback sorties. The first hint came to him from Aunty Kirra, an Aboriginal Elder who used to live near the mission where I was born. It turns out, she was my wet nurse. Then he did some detective work. And you know he's quite an A-lister when it comes to research. And guess what?'

We stood there – sister and brother – looking at each other in a quizzical sort of way. The same way we did all those years ago at Day Street. Brown on white skin. Blue eyes on blue.

ACKNOWLEDGEMENTS

Making Shadows had its beginnings not long after the passing of my brother Terry in 1984. Back then, I drafted the body of the story in a few short weeks. In a strange way, it helped me grieve for my best mate by temporarily immersing myself in the lives of other versions of 'me'. Indeed, each character is a raw measure of me, but then again, taken together, their combined stories have become something else: an integrated patchwork of 'selves' vacillating between light and dark.

The unfinished manuscript rested unresolved for almost forty years. By 2020, I had long retired from clinical practice, and was building upon a consuming interest in the humanities, specifically cultural semiotics. Changes in social habits during COVID prompted my wife, Jill, to suggest I finish the novel I'd started all those years ago. And that is what I did.

I am truly grateful to Kelly Rigby for her helpful suggestions following an initial reading of my draft manuscript. Subsequent advice and insightful editing by Kieran Devaney played a large part in enhancing the final form of the novel. Peter Long then helped convey the underlying theme of *war within peace* by his clever cover design.

In addition to my mentors, my thanks go to all those who have had to endure my ramblings about the process of writing a novel. And, importantly, I am indebted to my colleagues and staff at the Sydney Dental Hospital (previously, the United Dental Hospital of Sydney) and the Redfern Community Centre. Your support and commitment to the care and wellbeing of those you serve is inspirational.

www.ingramcontent.com/pod-product-compliance
Lightning Source LLC
Chambersburg PA
CBHW061057100726
47911CB00012B/276